CW01084170

Wolf of the Desert D

A Tale of Betrayal and Rebellion

By Edward Chilvers

Cover illustration by Nicola Chilvers

Published 2023

In the same series

Wolf of the Red Moon

Wolf of the Frozen North

Wolf of the Merchant City

Wolf of the Mystical Island

After journeying to the mysterious Volcano of the Lupine Dawn, ten year old Princess Aurnia of Cominaer receives the power of the Wolf of the Red Moon, a special ability gifted by the spirits of fate which allows her to turn into a powerful magical wolf whenever danger threatens. Joined by her guardian wolf, Lunar, Lunar's Uncle Fang, Goldenmane the pompous unicorn, Fenner the annoying porcupine, Hector the minotaur and Guselin the wicked frog Aurnia sets out on a series of exciting adventures to help the good people of the world and defeat evil wherever it rears its ugly head

Contents

Chapter One: The Oppressive Heat

"Naviphobia!" Exclaimed Fenner the porcupine with a flourish. "That's what I've got; it means a fear of boats if you care to ask."

"We don't," groaned Goldenmane the unicorn tiredly. "Now will you please stop being so annoying? I got next to no sleep last night."

"I don't know how you can all sit around being so causal," said Fenner worriedly. "Every ship we've ever sailed on has come to disaster and sank."

"There's only been two," said Princess Aurnia reasonably.

"Two!" Repeated Fenner. "There's some people who travel their whole lives on ships and they never sink once. Meanwhile we've had two ships sink on us and now we're on a third; it's a bad omen I tell you."

"We have to think positively," said Fang. Fang was an old grey wolf who had served as pack leader on their last four adventures. "So far the seas have been calm and there is no sign of danger."

"There was no sign of danger last time and we still found ourselves sucked into a whirlpool," muttered Fenner.

Lunar the grey wolf sidled up to Princess Aurnia and whined fearfully. She was an anxious and superstitious creature who disliked being at sea and didn't like to hear talk of sinking ships and bad omens. Aurnia put her arm around her friend to comfort her. Lunar's tongue was lolling out and she was panting heavily, for it was very hot on deck and the wooden ship seemed to radiate the heat. Not even opening the porthole windows seemed to make any difference.

Lunar decided she needed to get away from Fenner's annoying chatter. She went out on deck where a huge creature with the head of a bull was stood at the ship's wheel. "Hello Hector," panted Lunar as she slumped down on the deck in front of him. "Is there any sign of this heat letting up yet? Or a storm or some snow or a nice cool island with sheltered trees and high hills?"

"No such luck I'm afraid," replied the minotaur sadly. "Hey, if you're that hot why don't you go for a swim in the sea?"

"Ugh, no way," shuddered Lunar. "Wolves and saltwater don't mix and besides, I've had bad experiences of having to swim for my life in that sea."

Lunar got up slowly and made her way over to her water bowl in a shady spot beneath the sails. As she was preparing to drink a frog leapt out from beneath the surface and spat a huge jet of water right into her face.

"Ugh!" Cried Lunar, staggering back in horror. "Guselin, that is absolutely disgusting!"

"Aha! I got you!" Exclaimed the frog mockingly. "I have been waiting for you all morning and you walked straight into my trap; it was all part of my plan you know!"

"Oh yes?" Retorted the wolf. "And was this part of your plan too?" Lunar leaned forwards, picked Guselin up head first in her mouth and tossed him across the deck before starting to drink the water from her bowl.

"Idiot wolf!" Cried Guselin angrily. "I hope you are enjoying this heat! I did it you know! I am responsible! Oh yes! Aha! You will never escape!"

Lunar ignored the frog and carried on drinking. When she had finished she slumped down by the side of the deck and lay with her head on her paws. Lunar did not like being on this ship and she did not like the heat at all. Normally she was a very active creature who liked nothing better than scouting the forests around her home city of Talee in the kingdom of Cominaer. Just thinking of those forests made her feel very sad and she wondered if they would ever return there.

Princess Aurnia came out on deck and sat down beside Lunar. Lunar was Aurnia's guardian wolf who had taken a solemn oath to protect her; it was a promise the young wolf took very seriously and she possessed a deep bond with Aurnia too. An enchanted animal blessed with the power of speech who aged according to human years, she and the princess had been born on the same day under an auspicious moon with the ancient oracle Rina prophesising that their fates would be intertwined.

"I was just thinking about home," said Lunar sadly.

"I'm always thinking about home," sighed the princess. "How long have we been lost now? Weeks? Months? I've lost count."

"It seems like an age," sighed Lunar. "Your mum and dad must be so worried."

Aurnia nodded sadly as she thought about her parents, the king and queen of Cominaer. Even though her dad could be serious and strict and was always making her do boring maths and spellings she still missed him terribly just as she missed her mother's gentle touch and soft voice. She thought about the town of Talee with its happy, prosperous citizens and the well-kept streets and her home in the palace with the tapestries and huge windows, and she thought of the forest beyond where she liked to run and play with Lunar on the rare occasions her father allowed them to go scouting together.

"Why is it so hot, idiot princess?" Demanded Guselin as he came hopping across the deck to join them. "This is not acceptable; even hopping along the deck has the effect of frying the mighty Guselin's flippers!"

"I thought you said it was all because of you," said Lunar sarcastically. "All part of your plan didn't you say? Well if you made it so hot perhaps you could make it cold again?"

"Do not try to use my words against me, foolish wolf!" Snapped the frog crossly. "The mighty Guselin is an amphibian of riddles; you never know what he is going to do next, oh no!"

"But I do know what you're going to do next," said Aurnia simply. "You're going to hop into my knapsack and go to sleep."

"Pah! Shows what you know!" Retorted Guselin mockingly.

"Oh no?" Said the princess. "What are you going to do then?"

"Never you mind," replied the frog as he turned and began to hop towards the steps which led down into the cabins. "The mighty Guselin does not have to justify his actions to a mere underling like you! Right, where's that knapsack?"

After Guselin had hopped below deck Fang came to join them outside.

"How long has it been since we were sucked into that whirlpool, uncle?" Asked Lunar.

"Eight days today," replied the older wolf gravely. "Which in turn makes it two days since we left the island of Duddledor."

"Only two days?" Sighed Lunar. "It seems much longer. Well that's good in a way I suppose."

"And yet we still have no idea where we are or how to get home," muttered Lunar.

"Not quite," replied Fang. "Remember the mermaid king told us to head south to a land called Firehara? He said there was a great city there with merchants from all over the world. Somebody there must know how to get back to Cominaer."

"But when do we get to Firehara?" Sighed Lunar. "And what else will we find when we get there? Nothing is ever straightforward with us. Everywhere we go we always seem to fall into a dangerous adventure."

"What are you talking about? Adventures are loads of fun!" Exclaimed Fenner as he came to join them on deck. "I absolutely love adventures; I can't wait until our next one!"

"Isn't this an adventure in itself then?" Asked Lunar.

"Being on this ship you mean? Not in itself, no," replied Fenner. "This is sort of like the bit before the adventure when we set the scene and promise ourselves we're going to have an easy time of it and everything will be fine. Then something dramatic happens and boom! Off we go on yet another adventure."

"Well you're certainly in a better mood all of a sudden I must say," said Aurnia.

"That's right," smiled Fenner. "I've had a brainwave!"

"What do you mean?" Asked Lunar. "And hey, what have you got there?"

Aurnia and Lunar saw that Fenner was carrying a can and a paintbrush in his paws. Fenner grinned. "I've worked out why all the ships we sail on keep sinking — it's because they don't have names! Don't you know it's a bad omen for a ship not to have a name?"

"Actually no I didn't know that," replied Lunar.

"Well now you do and it's true," said Fenner with a flourish. "So that's what I'm going to do now — give this ship a name." Fenner went over to a long coil of rope, picked it up and tied one end to the mast of the ship and the other end around his waist.

"Hey, shouldn't we consult on this?" Called Aurnia as Fenner began to swing himself over the side of the ship with the paint pot and brush in his paws. "I mean naming a ship is a pretty big thing you know."

"Don't worry, I know exactly what I'm doing," called Fenner as he vanished out of sight. "I'm going to name it after Lord Goldenmane."

At that moment Goldenmane himself trotted up the steps and joined them on deck. The unicorn was pompous, arrogant and extremely full of himself but he was also a loyal and noble creature who never hesitated to put himself in danger for the good of his friends.

"It is becoming hotter by the minute!" Exclaimed the unicorn angrily, addressing Hector as though it was all his fault. "What were you thinking sailing us directly into this – this heat-storm?"

"The instructions from the mermaid king and queen were that we were to sail south," replied Hector reasonably. "I'm just doing as they said."

"Pah! What would a common mermaid know?" Snapped the unicorn crossly. "Conditions on this ship are becoming quite unbearable. How could there be anyone living even close to this heat, let alone an entire city of merchants?" He wandered over to the side and looked down in surprise. "What's that porcupine hanging over the side with the paintbrush for?"

"He's decided to name the ship," replied Lunar. "In fact he's decided to name it after you."

"He's what?" Thundered Goldenmane furiously.

"Aren't you happy?" Said Aurnia in surprise. "I thought you'd be honoured."

"But this is Fenner we're talking about here!" Cried Goldenmane. "He's not going to name the ship 'The Lord Goldenmane' or "The Noble Unicorn,' he's going to name it something that annoys me like 'The Horse,' an animal to which you know I hate to be compared, or 'The Blustering Idiot," which he is always calling me."

"Oh come on now Goldenmane I'm sure it will be fine," said Fang encouragingly.

"At that moment Fenner climbed back over the side of the ship and set down the paintbrush. "It is done!" He declared triumphantly. "The ship has a name at last."

"What did you call it?" Asked Aurnia nervously.

"The Horned Donkey!" Replied Fenner happily.

"Well of course you did!" Whinnied Goldenmane crossly as he began to stomp his way back to his cabin. "I have never met such an annoying creature in all my life. What business common tundra porcupines have talking at all is quite beyond me!"

Chapter Two: The Desert Land

That afternoon it became hotter still. Aurnia was wearing a light pair of shorts and t-shirt but it was still far too hot. Hector had the novel idea of hauling buckets of seawater on board the ship and pouring them into Goldenmane's trough so that Fenner and the wolves at least could roll around in it and cool down. Goldenmane of course complained bitterly but although he didn't like to admit it he was suffering less than most of the others because as a sort of horse he was able to cool himself down by drinking the freshwater in the other trough he kept in his personal cabin.

Aurnia decided to go up to the crow's nest, partly because Fenner was being exceedingly annoying and partly because she was hoping it would be cooler up there in the fresh air. In this last point she was disappointed. There was barely any wind at all and now she didn't even have the shade of the sails to cool her. She pulled a wide brimmed hat over her head and looked out. The sea shimmered in the heat and the horizon ahead of her was blurred.

"Ahoy there, young princess!" Said Fenner jovially as he climbed up into the crows nest to join her.

Aurnia was tempted to say the only reason she had come up here in the first place was to get away from him but that would have been very mean even if Fenner had been exceptionally annoying that morning. So instead she smiled and said; "Oh hello Fenner, how nice to see you."

"What can you see apart from the sea?" Asked Fenner before bursting out laughing at his own joke.

Aurnia turned and squinted ahead of her although the sun was very bright and reflected off the water. There was a small patch of grey on the horizon but it might just have been the light playing tricks on her. "I'd like to think I might be able to see something," she said. "But in this heat everything shimmers so much and it is always so bright. I find the best times to look are either sunrise or sunset when the light isn't so intense and the temperature is cooler."

"I know what you mean," agreed the porcupine. "As the official ship's lookout even I'm getting bored being up here all the time. There's been nothing for days, not even a passing porpoise."

Aurnia looked again at the patch of grey. It looked a little more pronounced now. "Hey," she said hopefully. "That might be something after all."

Fenner leaned over the railing and looked hard. "You might be right," he said excitedly. The porcupine and the princess waited for a few minutes until they saw the definite outline of hills. "It is!" Cried Fenner, leaping up and down in delight. "Land ho! Land ho!" He called down to Hector. "Land ho, Hector! Twenty-five degrees starboard!"

"Land ho? Righty ho," replied Hector as he began to steer the ship to starboard.

"Twenty-five degrees starboard? How did you know to say that?" Asked Aurnia.

"Oh I didn't," replied Hector casually. "But it sounds rather clever don't you think?"

As if anticipating land the ship's sails picked up a sudden gust of wind and began to speed south towards the hills. The others came out on deck to see what all the fuss was about as Aurnia and Fenner slid down the rigging to join them. "Land at last!" Exclaimed Lunar happily. "I'll be glad to set my paws on hard ground let me tell you."

"Where do you think we are?" Said Fenner. "Maybe we'll find we aren't too far from home after all."

"I wouldn't be so sure about that," said Fang as he leaned over the deck and looked closely. "Come and see for yourself. Those aren't hills, they're sand dunes."

Aurnia and her friends came to the front of the deck and saw it was true. Huge mountains of fine orange sand confronted them and as they came closer they saw that the land filled the horizon as far as they could see. "If this is an island it must be truly massive," said Fang.

"Massive and hot," added Fenner. "A huge desert island. I wonder if anyone lives there?"

"Well I have never heard of a desert island with such large sand dunes," said Goldenmane, who was very well versed on geography. "I'm afraid this isn't any place in the known world."

"Not in the world we know maybe but remember the mermaids said this desert land was home to a thriving civilisation," said Fang. "This has to be Firehara."

"But remember the mermaids also said the people of Firehara were a little strange," said Fenner worriedly.

"Strange or not this is the first land we have seen for days and we have to investigate," said the older wolf. He turned to Hector. "Let's sail in close," he said. "We will make anchor at the first port we see."

One hour later the ship was sailing alongside the island, so close that Aurnia could see the huge sand dunes looming above them. In places the wind was swirling the sand around to create small storms of dust. There were no beaches to speak of, for the dunes came right up to the sea and plunged down into the water, which had been turned orangey brown by the sand. Although Aurnia and her friends looked closely they could not make out another living thing on the land before them. There was nothing but sand.

"So much for finding a port," said Fenner in disappointment.

"I wonder if anyone lives here at all," said Lunar.

"Well of course nobody lives here, how could they?" Demanded Goldenmane pompously. "Why the place is clearly uninhabitable. There is nothing to eat and the shifting sands would not even allow for anything to be built. What a truly wretched place."

"But the mermaids said we would find a thriving civilisation here," said Lunar.

"Pah! What do mermaids know?" Scoffed Goldenmane. "It just goes to show you can't trust common creatures to tell you anything right!"

But if there's nobody here who can we go to for help?" Asked Aurnia worriedly. "We can't keep sailing around forever."

"Aha! But that is exactly what you'll do!" Laughed Guelin as he leapt up on to the deck and started to dance around on his hind legs whilst waving his front flippers in the air. "Look at this horrible sandy place; isn't it awful? Well guess what? I did this! It was all part of my plan!"

"Does it not occur to you, awful creature that you are, that whatever happens to us also happens to you?" Snapped Goldenmane irritably.

"Indeed not idiot horse!" Taunted Guselin. "For I am a creature of the desert; I thrive in these sorts of conditions."

"You must certainly do not thrive in these sorts of conditions," retorted Aurnia as the unicorn whinnied indignantly. "You are a frog and as such your natural habitat is a cool wet swamp. There is nothing like that here. If you stay here too long your skin will dry out and you will have nothing to eat. You can't drink the saltwater or even swim in it and you can't eat sand either."

"Do not underestimate the mighty Guselin!" Snapped the frog crossly.

"Oh just go away and take a nap will you?" Sighed Lunar in exasperation.

"Aha! I shall!" Laughed Guselin, and with that he hopped away to find the knapsack pocket.

Hector sailed the ship alongside the sand dunes for a long time. Nothing changed in the scenery at all although the friends watched the land closely, desperately trying to spot signs of life. When the sun went down the wind kicked up the sand which swirled around them and got into their eyes.

"Enough!" Cried Fang as he put his head down and hurried for shelter. "Let's just anchor here for the night and resume tomorrow when this dust storm subsides."

Hector hastily lowered the anchor as Aurnia and her friends hurried below deck. The minotaur joined them a moment later and they huddled together in the dining room as the dust storm gathered in intensity. When Aurnia looked out of the porthole all she could see was a hail of sand whizzing past and rattling on the glass. Even though the porthole was closed tightly some of the sand still managed to find its way inside.

"What a horrible, awful part of the world!" Exclaimed Goldenmane fearfully. "Why don't we just turn around and head back to Duddledoor Island? At least there are people there."

"And beaches," said Fenner.

"And forests," added Lunar wistfully.

"We are too far from Duddledoor Island to go back there now," said Fang reasonably. "I agree this land has been disappointing so far but I do not think the mermaids have lied to us. The civilisation of Firehara must be around here somewhere. We will find it eventually."

"If we're not buried in the sand along with this ship!" Exclaimed Goldenmane dramatically.

After dinner Aurnia and Lunar went off to their cabin. Aurnia got into bed whilst Lunar lay down in her basket. The sandstorm continued unabated, rattling the windows as it swirled around them. The princess was very glad she was in her cabin and not outside on deck or stuck amidst the sand dunes. She wondered what tomorrow would bring and whether they would ever find the fabled land of Firehara the mermaids had urged them to head for.

Chapter Three: One Flower

Aurnia slept badly that night because it was very hot in the cabin and awoke early the next morning just as the sun was coming up. Wearily she got out of bed and got changed. Lunar got up too and joined her as they went up on deck. The sandstorm had passed but had left its mark on the ship. Sand was piled high all over the ship, drifting against the side of the deck so that it came up to

Aurnia's knees in places. In fact just about every single surface of the ship was covered in sand. Aurnia picked some of it up and let it run through her fingers. The sand was very fine and light and not at all like the sand to be found on the beaches back home.

"Hey, look at this," said Fenner as he came to join them on deck. "One of us had better get sweeping huh?"

After breakfast Hector came out on deck and hauled up the sails. As he did so a great concentration of sand came raining down and forced Aurnia and Lunar to dive for cover. As the minotaur pulled up the anchor to get them moving again the sand started to fall from the surfaces and they were once more forced to shield their eyes until it had passed.

For the next two hours the ship crawled along the coastline. The scenery hardly changed at all; nothing but tall sand dunes as far as the eye could see.

"Hey!" Exclaimed Fenner excitedly. "Look over there!"

Aurnia looked and saw a small spindly green plant growing up from the sand.

"Well I never," scoffed Goldenmane. "Imagine getting so excited over a mere plant."

"Hey, it's life isn't it?" Retorted Fenner. "The first we've seen on this land since we got close."

"Fenner is right," said Fang. "If plants are growing around these parts it means the land is becoming more hospitable. The more hospitable the land the greater the chances of finding life."

The ship continued along its course along the straight coastline. More plants popped up between the sand and the colour of the sand itself changed from a dry orange to a muddy brown. As Hector steered the ship around a narrow peninsula they caught sight of a river estuary surrounded by a bay. Here the land exploded with life. Plants of all colours and sizes grew amidst the flat and rocky land and there was even a beach. This was, however, only a brief area of life, for all around the bay the sand dunes loomed once more.

"Hey!" Cried Fenner excitedly. "Is that a hut I see?"

They looked and saw a small shack perched on a patch of raised ground just above the river.

"It is!" Said Aurnia. "And look, there's a wisp of smoke coming from the chimney. That's means there's somebody home."

"Yes, and there will be a place to weigh anchor in the river," said Hector as he turned the wheel starboard.

"Only one mud hut," muttered Goldenmane as they began to sail up the river. "So much for the mighty trading civilisation of Firehara. This place looked pretty common to me."

Aurnia went to her cabin and made ready to land. She packed a few things into her knapsack then picked up the staff that had been lying beside her bed. The staff glowed at the top as Aurnia touched it, reacting to her power as the Wolf of the Red Moon. She had obtained the staff back on Duddledoor Island from an evil wizard and although she didn't quite understand its full power she had managed to master a few spells that had saved their lives on more than one occasion. Aurnia was a little afraid of the staff's power and hoped they did not have to use it but she was going to take it with her just in case.

Hector found a good spot in the river and with Aurnia and Fenner's help he took down the sails and lowered the anchor before hauling out the gangplank to allow them to disembark. Lunar trotted on to the muddy foreshore, wagging her tail as she went. "Land at last!" She exclaimed happily. "How good it feels to finally set my feet on dry land."

As Aurnia made her way on to the bank Guselin leapt out of her knapsack and started hopping around in the mud. "Aha! Paradise!" He exclaimed happily. "All part of my plan. Oh yes!"

Once they had all disembarked Aurnia looked around. It was not a very inspiring setting. The river was muddy and what few plants there were stood spindly and bent over. The cottage itself appeared very ramshackle and then there was the desert which loomed all around. "I wonder who lives there?" She said, pointing at the shack.

"There's only one way to find out," replied Fang. "Come along, let's go and introduce ourselves."

"Are you coming Guselin?" Asked Aurnia as the frog continued hoping about in the puddles.

"Indeed not, you are all doomed!" Retorted Guselin defiantly. "You shall go and meet your ultimate destruction whilst I, the mighty Guselin, shall remain here in my new domain over which I shall soon reign supreme! Oh yes!"

Guselin hopped along the water's edge, his face smug and conceited. All of a sudden the water exploded around him. A medium sized yellow snake lunged out of the river straight towards him and snapped at him with its powerful fangs, missing him by mere inches.

"Oh no!" Cried the frog in horror as he turned and tried to hop away. "Help me! Help me!"

The snake lunged again but just as its jaws were about to close around the frog, Lunar leapt through the air and caught its body in her mouth, twisting and snarling as she mauled it back and forth before tossing it far into the river. The snake turned and dived down beneath the muddy depths as the terrified Guselin hopped back to Aurnia who picked him up and popped him into the knapsack pocket.

"Thank goodness for Lunar," said Aurnia in relief. "Without her you would have been serpent food. Let that be a lesson not to hop around in a strange place and lose sight of your friends."

"That stupid wolf did nothing!" Declared Guselin defiantly. "I fought off that snake myself; the mighty Guselin cannot be defeated! Aha!"

"What nonsense," retorted Fang crossly. "The least you could do is be grateful. Lunar put herself at considerable risk taking on that snake. She might have been seriously hurt."

"Aha! So the snake I sent almost succeeded huh?" Taunted Guselin. "Next time the idiot wolf will not be so lucky!"

As the discourteous frog settled back into the bottom of Aurnia's knapsack for yet another nap the princess and her friends headed up to the shack at the top of the riverbank. Up close the shack was even more ramshackle than it had appeared from the sea. It appeared to have been built of scavenged driftwood and there were several holes in the wall that seemed to have been patched up with mud from the river.

"What a curious place," said Aurnia.

"What a common place," muttered Goldenmane. "Us unicorns wouldn't use a place like this as a tool-shed!"

Aurnia took a deep breath, stepped up to the door and knocked firmly before stepping back, holding her staff tightly in case she had to use it. Lunar and Fang came to stand beside her, ready to leap at the first sign of danger.

"Huh? What?" Came a voice from within. "Look friend, I don't have it just now; I just need a little more time to get it, okay?"

Aurnia and her friends looked at one another. The princess knocked again. There was silence. "Hello?" Said Aurnia.

"Nobody home!" Came the voice from within.

"There quite clearly is somebody home," retorted Goldenmane pompously. "Open this door right now, my man!"

There came another long silence followed by the sound of something being knocked over. Stumbling footsteps approached and the door opened a crack. A long nose not dissimilar to that of a horse peered out at them.

"Woah!" Exclaimed the voice in alarm. "This can't be for real!"

"I can assure you we are very real," declared Goldenmane. "Now stop messing around and open this door."

There came a heavy sigh and a moment later the door was flung open. Before them stood a most unusual creature. Its head was shaped like that of a horse with yellow fur and it had a huge snout with flaring nostrils, jutting front teeth and large black eyes. Its body was like that of a human's only it had a pronounced hump on its back. The creature was dressed in colourful multi-dyed shirt and brown cloth trousers and had huge flat feet.

Everyone except Fang took a step back and gasped. The older wolf however smiled and bowed politely. "Please forgive my friends," he said pleasantly. "Clearly they have never met a camelolean before."

The camelolean looked at them in alarm. "What do you want?" He demanded. "Are you from the bank? Look, I told you I'll get the money, I'm just waiting for my investments to pay off. You're going to have to give me some time, guys. I mean come on!" He threw his hands into the air appealingly.

"Oh no you're quite mistaken," said Aurnia reassuringly. "We're not from the bank at all; we're a party of lost adventurers trying to find our way home. You haven't heard of the kingdom of Cominaer by any chance have you?"

"Probably, probably," replied the camelolean vaguely. "I've forgotten a lot of things. So you're definitely not from the bank then?"

"Definitely not," replied Aurnia.

"Really good, really good," muttered the camelolean. "Well hey, I'm always happy to make new friends. If you're stuck for something to do why not stick around with me for a while? I mean I don't have much but I could probably make you up a nettle soup or something."

"Don't you have any gold leaf infused hay?" Asked Goldenmane rudely.

"Do I look like a guy who carries around gold leaf to sprinkle on hay?" Replied the camelolean.

"Ah no, perhaps not," acknowledged the unicorn.

The inside of the camelolean's shack was no less chaotic than the outside. The windows were covered over with ragged dirty fabric to serve as curtains whilst the furniture was battered and in a very poor state of repair. A filthy brown carpet covered the floor and there was paint peeling off the walls. The corners of the shack were cluttered up with broken pots and pans and there was a rickety table containing an unwashed bowl and cup.

"Come in, come in, make yourself at home," said the camelolean casually as he led the way inside. "My name is One Flower by the way. You can tell me all your names if you like but I'll probably forget so don't be offended." He turned to look at them and seemed somewhat taken aback. "Wow, I can't remember the last time I saw so many people."

"Don't you get many visitors around here then?" Asked Aurnia.

"Oh no, not around these parts and usually that's a good thing," replied One Flower. "I used to live in the big city and I can't say I got along too well. I didn't like the people there and they didn't like me. Also I ended up owing some of them a lot of money."

"You lived in the city?" Said Lunar. "Would that be the city of Firehara by any chance?"

"The very same," replied One Flower as he sat down heavily on a creaking armchair. "To tell you the truth I was glad to get out of there which was just as well because they didn't give me much choice."

"And you like living around here?" Said Goldenmane in disgust. "Living like this I mean?"

"Why sure I like it," replied One Flower with a smile. "I've got everything I need right here. The sheltered valley protects me from the desert heat, there's plants growing nearby for me to eat and I've got all the water I need in the river. Also, not many people know I'm here so my creditors don't know where to find me."

One Flower got up and lit a fire in the hearth and began to boil up some soup. He handed out some rags for Aurnia and her friends to sit on and they made themselves as comfortable as possible on the floor. Goldenmane continued to look around the room in horror. He was a very clean and fussy sort of animal and he detested any kind of clutter.

"You say you used to live in Firehara," said Fang. "We are looking to reach that city to see if anyone knows how we might return home."

"Oh I wouldn't, really I wouldn't," replied One Flower vaguely. "For a start its so far and you have to walk right across the desert to reach it. Secondly there's the people. I mean some of them are alright but the sultan – he's a really uptight guy, you know? As for the banks..." He sighed and shook his head.

"Nevertheless we need to get there," said Fang. "If you know the way perhaps you could act as our guide?"

"Me? No way!" Exclaimed One Flower, shaking his head vigorously. "Haven't you heard me, wolf-friend? I've got people looking for me. I owe them money."

"It can't be very nice having to hide away from people all the time," said Aurnia reasonably. "Perhaps if you would agree to accompany us we could find a way to cancel your debts?"

"That's a nice thought but I don't see how you could," replied One Flower with a shrug. "I mean I'm guessing you've not got a lot of money, right?"

"Sadly not," admitted Aurnia.

"Then I really don't see what you could do," sighed One Flower. "They're pretty strict on debt repayment down in Firehara. Like I say, the Sultan is a pretty serious guy."

"Out of interest what exactly did you do with the money you borrowed?" Asked Goldenmane. "Because it certainly wasn't spent on the upkeep or maintenance of this shack."

"Like I say, things are pretty stern in Firehara," said One Flower as he began to dish the soup into various cracked bowls. "When you're an easy-going guy like me who just wants to live life as he pleases it isn't hard to fall foul of the law in a place like that. Let's just say I got myself into a little trouble and ended up taking out a loan to bribe a certain official into letting me go free."

"Oh great," muttered Goldenmane. "Not only are we in the company of a debtor, he's also a common crook to boot."

"Don't be so judgemental, Goldenmane," scolded Aurnia. "We've fallen foul of the authorities ourselves on more than one occasion during our various adventures."

One Flower handed out the soup. It didn't smell very good and it tasted even worse. Aurnia and the wolves grimaced as she swallowed it down whilst Fenner choked and coughed and Hector took one mouthful and discreetly put the bowl to one side, declining to eat anymore.

"I'll admit its an acquired taste," said One Flower apologetically. "But those desert nettles are the only food that grows in this valley."

There came the sound of greedy slurping. Aurnia turned around to look see Goldenmane delightedly finishing up his bowl. "Well!" He exclaimed approvingly. "One Flower may be a rather unorthodox sort of fellow but there's no denying he makes a good soup. Is there any more?"

"Here," said Hector, pushing his bowl across. "Why don't you have mine?"

"Don't mind if I do," said Goldenmane as he began to eat hungrily once more.

"Just like a horse to have strange tastes," said Fenner with a shake of his head. "Still, what can you expect from a creature that eats grass and hay?"

"Insolent animal!" Snapped Goldename crossly. "Why this must be the first time I've ever seen you turn down food. Oh well, all the more for me."

Chapter Four: Out Into The Desert

After dinner, One Flower brewed up some very strong and sweet black tea which was far tastier than the soup he had just served up to them. Aurnia and her friends sat around in a circle telling the camelolean all about their previous adventures and how they had come to be here in this desert land.

"Well it certainly sounds as though you've had a heavy time of it," said One Flower with a sad shake of his head. "All this anger and conflict in the world. Why can't we just come together and live in peace, that's what I want to know?"

"So all we want to do now is get home," said Fang. "If Firehara is a merchant city it must be visited by people from all over the world. One of them must know how to get back to Cominaer. We have to go there."

One Flower groaned and put his head in his hands. "You're conflicting me, wolf-friend," he groaned in anguish. "Why do you have to lay this all on me?"

"What do you mean?" Asked Fang.

"Just that the road to Firehara is rough and fraught with danger," replied the camelolean. "In fact there isn't a road from here at all, you have to go right across the sand dunes and there's all kinds of weird little creatures just waiting to spring out and do you damage. You'll never make it without a guide. At best you'll lose your way and wander around in the sands forever; at worst – no hang on, that was the worst. Oh dear oh dear. I'm going to have to come with you after all aren't I? what choice to I have? There's this ancient tribal camelolean code to never leave a traveller behind in the desert. I've got to do my duty; I don't have a choice. Oh man!"

"Well don't sound too enthusiastic about it," muttered Goldenmane sarcastically.

"We'd really appreciate your help," said Lunar kindly. "And even if people are after you for money I'm sure we could talk to the sultan and get something arranged."

"Indeed so," replied Goldenmane primly. "I myself am an excellent negotiator. I'm sure the sultan would be so honoured to be in the presence of one from the unicorn tribe he would agree to forgo your debt straight away no sooner I asked him to do so."

"Maybe you could, I don't know though," shrugged One Flower. "I think maybe I'll just get you within sight of the city and make my own way back. You all seem like experienced adventurers, I'm sure you'll be fine handling yourself when you get there.

The friends spent the night in One Flower's shack before setting off, because the camelolean wanted to get an early start so they could avoid the beating sun as much as possible. It was a couple of hours before dawn when Aurnia woke up. One Flower was already up and about getting supplies ready for the journey ahead. Aurnia noticed he had filled four large barrels with water from the nearby pump. "Will we really need all that water?" She asked him.

"Will you need it? I don't think it will be enough," replied One Flower. "You don't know how hot it gets out there on the dunes; we're going to have to find an oasis or something to stock up again."

When the others got up, One Flower reached into a battered old chest and took out a heap of what looked like brown sacks alongside some ragged slippers of varying sizes and shapes. "You're going to need these to keep the heat off your backs," he said. "Especially you wolves with all that fur whilst the slippers will prevent your feet from becoming too hot in the sand."

Aurnia pulled one of the sacks over her head and down to her feet. It was itchy and heavy and the hood came down too far over her eyes but when she stepped outside she was glad of it, for it reflected the rays of the sun and provided some protection against the intense heat.

Aurnia's sack was the only one that fitted. All of the others had to be cut down to size and tailored to suit the shapes of the various animals. Goldenmane, of course, complained bitterly at having to wear such an undignified garment but then again, thought Aurnia, he would have complained about the sun and the heat as well so there really was no pleasing him.

"We do look strange," said Aurnia as One Flower and Hector loaded the water barrels onto Goldenmane's saddlebags and prepared to set off.

"Strange that we have to wrap up in the desert just as much as we do when we're adventuring out in the cold snowy forests," quipped Fenner. "I sort of like it though, especially the hood. Very cloak and dagger don't you think?"

"This is all so undignified," muttered Goldenmane crossly as he stamped his feet impatiently. "Not only do I have to dress up in these ridiculous garments, I am also expected to carry the load – yet again!"

"It is only natural you should carry the heavy load," said Fenner cheerfully. "After all you are a..."

"A sort of horse!" Cried Goldenmane angrily. "That's what you're going to say, isn't it? You're going to compare me to a horse or a pack pony or a donkey or any other common equine just to needle me when I'm doing everything I can to help you!"

"Actually I was going to say you are a fine fellow who would do anything for your friends but if that's the way you're going to act I won't bother," said Fenner piously.

"You weren't going to say that and you know it!" Snapped the unicorn crossly.

"I can't get used to wearing shoes," said Lunar worriedly as she looked down at the slippers covering her feet. My paws are not only for walking, they're also a weapon against danger.

How will I be able to defend the princess when I cannot make use of my claws?"

"Let's hope that doesn't happen," said Fang as they made their way outside.

"Yes we'll be fine," replied Fenner casually. "The only thing we have to worry about is this heat. There's not going to be anyone silly enough to be lurking around in this desert heat to ambush us."

One Flower made a final check around his shack before locking the door behind him. "Yes, because you wouldn't want anyone to break in and steal any of your valuable items," said Goldenmane sarcastically. The camelolean carried with him a stout stick but was otherwise dressed in his normal clothes, for he was a creature who was used to these conditions and the hump on his back kept him supplied with water for many days in advance.

"So here we go again!" Exclaimed Fenner happily as he skipped ahead of them. "Off on another adventure; how exciting!"

The friends left the shack and the river behind them and climbed up the valley until they stood on a small hill overlooking the desert. Ahead of them were endless sand dunes stretching as far as the eye could see. The heat hit their faces as though they were standing right in front of a roaring fire. Aurnia sighed and pulled her hood down over her face. She did not envy Lunar and Fang with their thick coats and just hoped they could make the journey in one piece. They headed down the hill and stepped onto the sand. It was very fine and soft and sank around their feet, making the going difficult and taxing the muscles in their legs. Aurnia put her head down and pushed ahead but despite her robe and hood the sun was very hot and beat down oppressively. She began to puff and pant, her legs aching as she continued, the heat sapping her strength. The others were having similar problems. Fenner's little legs were totally unequipped to handle the sand and he kept slipping and falling. Eventually, he had to go on Goldenmane's back which the unicorn was not happy about at all. Lunar and Fang puffed and panted and walked slowly, unable to trot ahead and scout as they usually did. Hector flared his nostrils and pushed on as best he could but because he was a larger creature his walk became lumbering and he staggered. Goldenmane, although he complained far more than anyone else, was actually less affected, his wide hooves allowing him to cross the sand far easier than Aurnia with her smaller human feet. One Flower walked ahead singing and whistling an upbeat tune. He was after all in his natural camelolean habitat.

Guselin poked his head out of Aurnia's knapsack pocket. "Aha! Where are we? Yes! All part of my plan!" He exclaimed as he looked around. "Why is it so hot, idiot princess? What is this place?"

"We are crossing the desert towards Firehara," replied Aurnia disinterestedly.

"Ah yes! I remember now!" Replied the frog. "Once this desert consisted of fertile fields and gently rolling countryside. Then I, the mighty Guselin appeared and wrought havoc upon the land, turning the lush meadows to desert and sending the hapless people to their doom! Now you, my foolish enemies, are cursed to wander this barren land forever whilst I rule over you all. Aha! Yes! This forsaken land is mine I tell you!"

Guselin leapt out of the knapsack and onto the sand which was dry, gritty and very hot indeed. Needless to say, these were hardly ideal conditions for an amphibian and the frog immediately began to hop up and down and cry out. "Aargh! It burns! It's too hot!" He cried out in panic. "Help me! Help me!"

Aurnia quickly scooped the frog up, took her flask and poured a generous amount of water over his body to rehydrate him. "It hurts!" Moaned Guselin. "More water!"

"You know there's an old human saying that says 'look before you leap,'" said Aurnia as she slipped him back into her knapsack pocket. "Maybe you should learn from it. That's the second time this adventure somebody has had to rescue you from your own foolishness. You are *precipitous,* Guselin. It means to act rashly or too quickly."

"Aha! I know full well what *perpendicular* means!" Snapped the frog angrily. "Do not patronise me, idiot princess, the mighty Guselin is always one step ahead of the game. Even when he is seen to act foolishly it is actually a fiendish double bluff – all part of my plan you know!"

As Guselin settled back down in the knapsack pocket, safely away from the sun's rays, and went back to sleep, Aurnia and her friends continued to battle against the fierce desert. A huge sand dune loomed before them. As they climbed the sand slipped beneath their feet and seemed to carry them backwards. It was only with great difficulty, and after a lot of time, that they finally reached the summit.

"Let's stop for a break!" Groaned Fenner even though he had been on Goldenmane's back the whole time and hadn't done any of the climbing at all. "I'm absolutely exhausted! We must have been walking for hours."

"It seems so but you'd be wrong," sighed Aurnia despairingly. "Look back there!"

The friends turned and looked behind them and saw, not too far away at all, the top of One Flower's cottage with a wisp of smoke still billowing out of the chimney. Beyond that was the sea and their ship, the *Horned Donkey,* resting peacefully at anchor in the river.

"Oh no!" Cried Goldenmane despairingly. "All that hard work and suffering and we're not even out of sight of our home base!"

Chapter Five: The Oasis

The friends pressed on across the desert and sand dunes. The sun beat down and it only seemed to get hotter as the day wore on. Every half an hour, sometimes sooner, they were forced to stop and drink from the wooden water barrels which Goldenmane was carrying. Whilst Aurnia, Fenner and Hector could drink straight from the barrels the others had to have their bowls and troughs unpacked and set down for them and then packed away again which delayed them further (One Flower, as a camelolean, hardly drank at all because he already had enough water stored up in his hump). To make matters worse Fenner then decided to sing.

"We're eight friends

Wandering lost in the desert

Its quite unpleasant

Oh! When will it end?

The bright sun

Beats down hot on our bent backs

The soft sand

Covers our tracks!

"Goodness me!" Groaned Aurnia. "You know, Fenner, it really would be far more pleasant if you didn't do that."

"What? I'm just trying to keep everybody's spirits up," replied Fenner innocently.

"That porcupine has too much energy," muttered Goldenmane. "I couldn't sing if I wanted to – in fact, it hurts my throat to talk but that's because I'm doing all the work carrying this porcupine *and* all the water and luggage."

"Talking of water I'm thirsty again," said Hector.

"Me too," said Lunar. "Can we stop again?"

"But we've only just stopped, friends" said One Flower. "We'll never get to Firehara if we have to keep resting up every five minutes."

"That's easy for you to say, you're a camelolean," retorted Goldenmane. He stopped in the sand. "Well, I refuse to go another step without some refreshment!"

"Hey," said Fenner worriedly as he turned the tap on the barrel. "This thing is empty."

"This one too," said Aurnia as she tried in vain to get water out of the barrel on the opposite side.

"And this one is only about a third full," said Hector.

"Oh no, you're kidding?" Said One Flower anxiously. "That water needs to be rationed, adventurer friends. We've not been gone two hours and most of the water is already gone. We've got another day and a half at least until we reach Firehara, even longer if we keep having to stop and rest."

"This is all Goldenmane's fault," said Fenner accusingly. "Every time we stop he fills up his trough. It's him who is drinking most of the water."

"It's me who is doing most of the work!" Cried Goldenmane indignantly. "You're drinking more than your fair share of water considering all you're doing is sitting on my back making up stupid songs to drive us all up the wall!"

"Never mind who is to blame, what are we going to do?" Asked Lunar. "We can't possibly travel for another two days with less than two barrels of water and it doesn't look as though this desert is going to cool down anytime soon."

"But it will!" Exclaimed Fang. "When the sun goes down at night we will be able to travel far easier."

"Of course!" Said Aurnia. "Why didn't we think of that before?"

One Flower raised his head and sniffed at the arid desert air. "If we want to travel at night we will need to find somewhere to rest up now," he said. "My camelolean senses tell me there's an oasis not far from here. It's another few hours of walking at least but we would need to go there anyway to restock our water supplies."

"Sounds great," said Fenner. "Another quick drink and we'll go."

"We need to go careful on the water as One Flower says," warned Fang. "Remember we have been caught out before. Let's save as much of the water as we can in case of an emergency."

The friends carried on walking across the shifting sands. The going remained tough but there was a new spring in their steps as they looked forward to reaching the oasis.

"Listen!" Exclaimed Lunar suddenly. "I can hear something."

Fang cocked his head and listened closely. "So can I," he said. "A creature of some sort but I can't think what kind."

"I can't hear a thing," said Aurnia. "I suppose your wolf hearing must be far better than mine."

"There's a few of them," said Lunar. "Sort of howling, but not like a wolf."

"No, too high-pitched to be a wolf," agreed her uncle. "But certainly a *canis* species of some sort."

"So you mean a sort of dog," said Fenner.

"Hey! How dare you compare me to a common dog!" Exclaimed Lunar indignantly.

"Now you know how I feel when Fenner teases me," muttered Goldenmane.

"The question is are they friendly?" Said Hector as he took his stout staff from around his back and held it close.

One Flower put his ear in the air and listened. Aurnia could hear it too now – a series of high-pitched barking howls floating across the sand dunes.

"Those are jackal friends," said One Flower said warily. "They're – how can I put it – a little territorial but they're not bad creatures really. I mean there are no bad creatures in this world, everyone just does what they do to survive but all the same – if we can hear them so close it must mean we're getting close to the oasis."

A high sand dune loomed before them and they struggled up it, the sand shifting against Aurnia's feet and going into her shoes. At the top of the sand dune they looked down and saw before them a wide parched valley stretching out into the distance. In the middle distance was a cluster of trees and greenery which formed a marked contrast to the otherwise lifeless landscape. A pool of clear blue water surrounded the trees. "There it is, friends!" Said One Flower proudly. "The oasis, just as I promised!"

"But look there," said Fang gravely as his eyes fell upon five four-legged creatures prowling around the oasis. "Those must be the jackals. They're territorial you say, One Flower? Well, that's fine, so are we wolves but we are always ready to assist those in need. Let's just hope our lupine cousins feel the same."

Aurnia and her friends set off down the slope of the sand dune towards the oasis. The jackals saw them and began to advance up the slope towards them. Aurnia thought they were curious-looking creatures: like wolves only smaller with brown and grey fur that went black on the back and very large ears that stuck up over their heads.

The alpha jackal stepped forwards. She was tall and slender with large amber eyes that glared suspiciously at the party as they came near. "My name is Whispera, pack leader of the jackal tribe," announced the alpha jackal. "What do you want? This is our oasis and we do not take kindly to strangers around here."

"We mean you no harm," said Fang, stepping forwards to address her. "We are on our way to Firehara and are tired and thirsty. We seek only to refresh ourselves at this oasis and rest until twilight when we shall continue our journey in cooler conditions."

Whispera snarled. "You are a strange-looking creature," she said warily. "Your ears are too short and your fur is too long."

"It is just the way the spirits made me," replied Fang diplomatically.

The jackal looked critically at Aurnia and her friends. "You are all rather strange in appearance," she muttered. "Especially your horse with that ugly-looking horn sticking right out of the middle of its head."

"Oh, how dare you!" Cried Goldenmane. "The audacity of a common sand-dwelling creature with ears as big as that to criticise my appearance!"

"Hush!" Hissed Aurnia quickly, but the jackal had heard the unicorn's words and was not happy.

"What did you say?" Demanded Whispera angrily. "You ask us for the use of our water supply and then you insult us?" The other jackals clustered around, the fur on their backs raised, their bodies pressed down ready to pounce.

"Now, now my jackal friends there's no need for the threat of violence," said One Flower appealingly. "We're all the spirit's creatures here, let's not wallow in our differences. We never meant to offend. All we are asking for is a cool drink of water and somewhere to rest."

"Perhaps," muttered Whispera thoughtfully. Her eyes narrowed. "But what will you give us in return?"

"Yes!" Exclaimed a younger jackal, coming to stand beside her. "What can you pay us?"

"Pay you?" Replied Aurnia. "I'm afraid we don't have a lot of money."

"Or any at all for that matter," added Fenner.

"No money, huh?" Muttered Whispera. "What about valuables?" She turned to the younger jackal. "It would appear as though our new friends are flat broke, Luxin."

"No money and no valuables either," said Aurnia. "But why would you need such things? You are wild animals, surely you don't buy or sell?"

That's where you're wrong," retorted Luxin. "You never know when you might need to enter into negotiations with Firehara, and in the human-run cities money talks."

"Yes, and if you don't have anything to give us we're not going to let you use our oasis," snapped Whispera.

"But that just isn't fair!" Cried Lunar angrily. "We are exhausted and thirsty and will struggle to survive unless we can have some water."

"That's just too bad," retorted Whispera carelessly.

"Too bad for you," snapped Goldenmane crossly. "There are only five of you and eight of us – well seven really because Guselin is a bit useless – but all the same we outnumber you and are clearly far stronger. We are going to drink and rest here whether you like it or not."

"But this is our oasis!" Cried Luxin angrily.

"And you can keep it," snapped Goldenmane. "We will be gone in a few hours just as soon as we have taken what we want."

"Peace, unicorn friend, peace!" Urged One Flower uncomfortably. "There's no need for confrontation here!"

"You're quite right," declared Goldenmane as he pushed past the outraged jackals and moved towards the oasis. "If these jackals just step aside and don't try to start any fights they can't win there's no need for a confrontation at all."

Fang hesitated for a moment then nodded. "Come along," he said to the others. "Let's go drink and rest."

"But what about the jackals?" Asked Lunar worriedly.

"Goldenmane is right in a way although he could have put it much better," said Fang. "We need to drink and rest. We cannot survive the rest of the journey unless we take refreshment at this oasis.

It might seem as though we're being the aggressor but this could be life or death for us."

"You will regret this!" Exclaimed Whispera angrily. She and the other jackals clustered together and followed the friends to the oasis before pausing at a safe distance. "You might think you are all civilised and above us but the creatures of the desert will not take kindly to such hostile acts of aggression. There will be consequences for this believe me!"

"We don't mean you any harm," said Aurnia, trying to sound reassuring. "We just want to have a drink and a rest beneath these trees."

"And we just want a little gold for the use of our property," snapped Luxin angrily.

"I told you," replied Aurnia. "We don't have any gold and we are not about to go thirsty just because we cannot pay for something that ought to be free regardless."

"Absolutely," stated Goldenmane pompously as he began to drink noisily from the water. "And besides, I'm sure this oasis was here long before you jackals."

"So was all land but it didn't stop you so-called civilised creatures building all over it and taking it for yourselves," snapped Whispera. "At least we have left this oasis as nature intended."

Guselin leapt out of the knapsack pocket and jumped into the oasis. "Aha!" He exclaimed. "Cool water at last! So we have taken this oasis over from the jackals, huh? Ah yes! All part of my plan!"

"You mean to say you were working for this frog all the time?" Asked Whispera in surprise.

"No absolutely not..." Began Aurnia.

"Aha! Oh yes! It is true!" Taunted Guselin as he leaned over the bank and blew a torrent of water at the jackals. "This place is mine now! Bow down to me and call me king and I might let you take a sip!" And with that the frog dived down into the water and began to swim around triumphantly, having the time of his life.

"This frog has no influence over us at all," said Aurnia flatly. "He is just my idiot pet."

"Be that as it may you are doing us a grave insult!" Cried Whispera. "There will be consequences you know!"

"Oh do be quiet you little runt!" Scoffed Goldenmane as he began to help himself to some succulent long grass at the edge of the oasis. "All your empty threats are putting me off my hard-earned meal!"

"Calling us runts, huh?" Muttered Whispera.

"Eating our grass, huh?" Added Luxin.

"All this anger and confrontation!" Exclaimed One Flower despairingly. "Why can't we all just live in harmony?"

Chapter Six: Pursuit Through The Desert

Aurnia slipped off her shoes and the uncomfortable robe that protected her from the heat of the desert, ran forwards and dived head-first into the oasis. The cold fresh water proved a wonderful shock after overheating for so long and she was deliriously happy and relieved as she kicked and splashed and swam back and forth. Lunar and the other animals came to join her, all except Fang who remained on the bank keeping a wary watch over the jackals, and One Flower, who watched the whole scene with amused interest (as a camelolean he had no need to cool down).

"It is good to cool down and get refreshed but I don't like that we just went and took what we wanted from the Jackals," said Lunar worriedly as she and Aurnia swam side by side. "I know they ought to have shared with us and we didn't really have a choice but all the same it doesn't feel right."

"I agree," said Aurnia. "Like you say we didn't have a choice but I never like to make enemies if I can help it."

Aurnia and her friends swam around and enjoyed the oasis for a long time before climbing out and having a long drink and something to eat. The desert sun dried them very quickly. Afterwards they went to lie beneath the shelter of a tall tree with overhanging branches and were soon fast asleep except for Lunar and Fang who remained awake to keep guard.

Lunar went and lay down in the shade of a patch of undergrowth a little way from the oasis. The jackals were watching them with faces of bitterness and anger, clustered together as they whispered amongst themselves. Lunar stared back at them, wondering how any wolf-like animal could deny other creatures food, water and shelter in the heat of the desert.

It was very hot in the desert despite the shade and the heat sapped Lunar's strength. She was very tired after the difficult journey through the desert and soon found herself yawning. The jackals continued to watch her but made no move. From her raised position she could see for miles. There was nothing else about, nothing else here except the seemingly endless sand.

Lunar's eyes grew heavy and before she knew it she had fallen asleep. She did not know how long she slept for but when she woke up with a start it was evening and the sun was starting to set over the dunes. She got up quickly and looked around. Aurnia, Fenner and One Flower were asleep under the shade. Hector and Goldenmane were close by at the oasis, the minotaur filling up the barrels of water and placing them into the unicorn's saddlebags ready to resume the journey that evening. A little way to the side of Lunar was Fang. He was sleeping too.

Lunar looked ahead. The jackals were still there but to her surprise there were only four of them now. She got up and looked across the desert then made a circuit of the oasis but there was no sign of the fifth jackal. She looked closer at the remaining four and saw it was the alpha female who was missing.

"Uncle Fang!" Said Lunar worriedly. "Wake up. We might have a problem here."

Fang opened his eyes and leapt to his feet. "Oh no!" He cried. "I can't believe I was caught napping. Am I... getting old?"

"Don't worry I was the same," Lunar reassured him. "It is just this heat. This is not our natural wolf habitat and we are suffering accordingly but that isn't what I wanted to talk to you about. It's the jackals. Whispera is missing."

"Missing? Are you sure?" Replied Fang.

"Quite sure," replied Lunar. "I have searched around the whole oasis but there is no sign."

"Who cares?" Muttered Goldenmane casually. "One less jackal means fewer of them to take on in a fight."

"I wouldn't be so sure of that," said Lunar, her eyes narrowing as she saw something on the far horizon. "It is as I feared; she is coming back with reinforcements!"

Fang hurried to her side and looked. In the distance, they saw the alpha jackal leading a much larger pack of at least twenty others coming towards them at a run. "Oh no!" Cried the older wolf. "Why did I let myself fall asleep?"

"We have to get out of here!" Said Lunar urgently. She ran to the shade of the tree and awakened the others with a series of loud and desperate barks. "Get up!" She commanded. "We have to run!"

Aurnia opened her eyes and leapt to her feet. She had no idea what was going on but she trusted her Guardian Wolf implicitly. If Lunar said they had to run that was all there was to it. She grabbed her knapsack and staff and turned around to see the pack of jackals racing towards them.

"Those who can get on my back!" Cried Goldenmane. Fenner and Aurnia leapt up onto Goldenmane's back whilst Lunar, Fang, Hector and One Flower ran alongside. The friends charged out of the oasis and began to rush across the desert away from the advancing jackals.

"It's no use!" Cried Fenner as he looked behind. "They're gaining on us!"

"Well of course they're gaining on us," whinnied Goldenmane. "It is this minotaur holding us up; I could run much faster if I didn't have to keep pace and protect him!"

"I'm running as fast as I can!" Panted Hector, but he was a creature built for strength not speed and it was true he could not run as fast as the others. Aurnia looked around and saw the jackals were getting close now. In a few seconds they would be upon them and then what would they do? She took a firm hold of her staff and concentrated hard. The light at the top began to glow with a greater intensity. The princess imagined in her mind's eye what she wanted to do and let out a cry, slashing a line across the air with the staff and sending lightning bolts of magic flying out. In a moment a huge wall of fire appeared between the friends and the jackals, turning night into day. The jackals skidded to a halt before the fire and looked at it in astonishment.

"What was that?" Cried Fenner in amazement.

"Never mind, let's just keep going until we lose them!" Urged Aurnia.

Goldenmane and the others on foot ran for all they were worth, over sand dunes and flat ground until at last Fang spied a rocky outcrop ahead of them. "Over there!" "He urged. "We can take stock and defend from those rocks if we need to."

"Wow you're really improving with that staff, Aurnia," said Fenner as he and the princess slid down from Goldenmane's back. Aurnia looked and saw the faint glow of the wall of fire in the far distance. It would not have delayed the jackals for very long but she hoped it would have deterred them from continuing with the chase at least.

"What common animals!" Panted Goldenmane angrily. "How dare they object to us using their oasis. Don't they realise it is a great honour for any animal to be in the presence of one from the unicorn tribe? Pah! No wonder they live out in the desert."

Guselin popped his head out of Aurnia's knapsack pocket. "Aha!" he exclaimed devilishly. "So the jackals I sent almost succeeded huh?"

"At least try to be consistent in your silly stories," sighed Aurnia. "Just this afternoon you were taunting the jackals and making even more trouble for us."

"Ah yes, it was a sophisticated double bluff you know!" Laughed Guselin. "I was merely pretending to be enemies with the jackals so I could bring about your doom. It was all part of my plan and you fell for it like the idiot you are. Oh yes! Aha!"

"If we fell for it why are we now safe and away from the jackals?" Asked Aurnia reasonably. "Aha! All part of you being an idiot."

"Do not mock me, foolish princess!" Snapped Guselin angrily. "One day I shall rule over you and when that time comes you can expect no mercy!" And with that he dived back down into the knapsack pocket and went straight back to sleep.

Fang climbed up on the rocks and looked out in the direction from which they had just come. "There is no sign of them but all the same we should make haste," he said. "We don't want to be out in this desert any longer than we have to be with those things prowling around."

"You want us to carry on? In the dark?" Said Hector worriedly. "What if they come back and ambush us?"

"Don't worry, Lunar and I will be on the alert," replied the older wolf. "We have to get to Firehara. As well as the threat of the jackals I don't want us to be out in the heat of the desert any longer than we have to be."

"Is it my imagination or is it sort of cold?" Said Fenner as they set off once more.

"Oh no, porcupine friend, it gets really cold in the desert at night," replied One Flower. "Its sort of magical, you know, how this is a land of contradictions."

"It is certainly not magical it is a huge pain in the neck!" Exclaimed Goldenmane with a shiver. "First it is too hot, then it is too cold and there is no happy medium at all. What a place to live; no wonder everyone we've met so far has been more than a little strange."

Lunar much preferred the cold to the heat and was in her element as she and her uncle scouted ahead, their ears pricked up and constantly alert for danger. Although the desert seemed largely barren and empty, Lunar's keen hearing and sharp sense of smell detected rodents scurrying back and forth around the sand dunes, bugs crawling around the rocks and lizards burrowing beneath their feet. What an amazing world it was, she thought to herself, that life could survive and even thrive in all types of varying climates.

Chapter Seven: Firehara

The friends pushed on through the night across the vast desert. The temperature dropped so low that Aurnia was forced to wrap the sack robe around herself to keep warm and found that her teeth were chattering. The animals, of course, were less affected by the cold although that didn't stop them from remarking on the sudden drop in temperature.

Several times through the night Lunar's keen lupine hearing made out the distant howls of jackals far away amongst the dunes. She looked worriedly across at Fang who shook his head; the jackals did not seem to be pursuing them so there was no need to alarm the others.

The friends walked quickly, eating and drinking along the way in the hope of making it to Firehara as quickly as possible. The huge sand dunes were dark and silent as they walked past and Aurnia thought they looked rather dramatic. Above them the full moon shone and the vast galaxy of stars beyond spread out in a dramatic canvas. Ahead of them Aurnia spotted the glimmers of dawn in the sky to the far east and not long afterwards a deep red glow was illuminating the sand dunes and the desert as the sun came up fast. As she scouted ahead, Lunar noticed changes in sound as the night animals returned to sleep and the day animals awoke to yet another blistering hot day. Not long after the sun had risen the rays were beating down and it became very hot once more.

"This is too much!" Groaned Goldenmane. "We have been walking through the night and I cannot go on much further."

"You won't need to, unicorn friend," said One Flower encouragingly. "Look there – the walls of Firehara lie before us!"

Aurnia and her friends looked up. There, shimmering through the heat, was a city in the middle of the desert. The city seemed to be built entirely of yellow stone which is probably why they had not seen it to begin with. It was surrounded with very high walls and beyond these walls Aurnia could make out flat roofed houses which seemed to stack one on top of each other like building blocks. Many of the buildings had balconies shaded with a multicoloured cloth awning overhead. There were domed temples and tall towers too and a large palace in the centre with golden coloured domes. The entrance into the city was via the most impressive set of gates

Aurnia had ever seen in her life. The gates were very tall and made of solid gold and on either side in front were a pair of huge seated lion statues with their mouths open, as if snarling a warning to those who arrived to make trouble.

"Well, this is as far as I go, friend," said One Flower as he eyed the city walls warily. "You know that place was home to me once but I can't say I miss it, not at all. You be careful when you go there, friends. Some of the folk are friendly enough but there are snakes as well – and I'm not talking about the slithering kind."

"What kind are you talking about then?" Asked Hector.

"The *people* kind," replied One Flower dramatically. "There's a lot of folk in Firehara out for whatever they can get which is exactly what the sultan wants, because whilst everyone distrusts one another he can do what he wants. That's why I went and lived in the wilderness, friends, to be away from all that. Just being within sight of these walls is giving me a bad feeling."

"Well, it's a shame you can't stay with us," said Lunar. "We could have done with somebody who knows the place to show us around the city."

"Oh, there's no way," replied One Flower with a shudder. "I can't ever go back behind those walls, not ever again."

Aurnia looked towards the gates and saw that they were opening. As she watched a contingent of around ten camelolean soldiers on horseback started out of the gates and began racing in their direction.

"What's happening?" Wondered Aurnia worriedly. "What could they want with us?"

"Oh no!" Cried One Flower in horror. "I've come too close. I'm in sight of the city gates and the watchmen must have seen me. Its too late! It's too late!"

"What's too late?" Asked Aurnia but at that moment the mounted cameloleans surrounded them. They were dressed in smart blue uniforms with wide brimmed hats to keep the sun out of their faces. At the sight of them, One Flower collapsed to the floor and curled up into a ball. The leader of the soldiers, a camelolean with gold braids on the shoulders of his uniform and a chest full of medals, came to loom over him with his horse.

"Aha!" Boomed the cameolean captain in an arrogant voice. "So you thought you were going to sneak back into the city did you?"

"Sneak back?" Squeaked One Flower in terror. "I don't know what you mean; I'm just a poor desert traveller, I've never been to the city once in my life before!"

"Indeed?" Laughed the captain. "So you deny your name is One Flower of Firehara? You say it is not your face featured on the wanted posters?"

"One Flower? Who's that?" Whimpered One Flower. "I don't know anyone of that name, Captain Anders! My name is – um – Two Cactus!"

The captain and the other soldiers looked at one another and smiled. "You are as bad at lying as you are at investing," said the captain harshly. "How, if you have never visited before, did you know my name is Captain Anders? We know who you are, One Flower, and we know the sultan will be very keen to become reacquainted with you."

"But what about his friends?" Said another soldier as he looked at Aurnia and the rest of the party.

"They're just ordinary travellers," said One Flower. "I was showing them the way to Firehara.

They've got nothing to do with this bother, believe me!"

Captain Anders considered for a moment as he scanned their faces. "Well, they're not on any wanted lists that I've seen," he muttered. "We could take them I suppose but why would we want to make any work for ourselves? What is your business here anyway?"

"My name is Princess Aurnia of Cominaer," said Aurnia. "We were carried here by a whirlpool from the other side of the world and are desperately seeking a way to get home. But please, sir, One Flower is our friend. We would never have gotten here without him. Is there nothing we can do to help him?"

"This wretch is at the sultan's mercy now," said Captain Anders sternly. "What happens to him next is not for me to decide."

"But we would like to see the sultan too," said Lunar. "We were hoping he might be able to help us return home."

The captain considered for a moment. "Well perhaps," he said, looking at Goldenmane. "It is not often we get unicorns here in Firehara and the sultan will doubtless be keen to make the acquaintance of such a noble and distinguished creature."

"Well of course!" Exclaimed Goldenmane delightedly, tossing back his long mane. "Your sultan sounds like a fine fellow already! If only everyone in this world had as much respect for the illustrious unicorn tribe!"

Four mounted cameloleans surrounded One Flower and forced him to march in step. Aurnia and her friends followed behind. Soon the great gates loomed before them, the stone lions huge and intimidating as they glared down.

Aurnia and her friends passed through the gates and into Firehara. For a city in the middle of the desert, there was a surprising amount of greenery. The city had been built around an oasis and there was an elaborate drainage system running alongside the sandstone streets which supplied water to the lawns and gardens. The streets were dusty and radiated heat, the citizens (mostly cameloleans) walking around in long hooded robes like the ones One Flower had given them. Merchant caravans were trundling back and forth along the streets and in the distance, Aurnia saw a crowded marketplace. The houses were large and looked well-maintained and the place gave an impression of wealth.

As they walked through the streets Aurnia slipped between the four horses escorting One Flower and came to walk side by side with the camelolean. "You said you owed somebody money but you didn't say that somebody was the sultan himself," said Aurnia. "Just what exactly did you do?"

"What did I do? I was trying to better myself, that's what!" Exclaimed One Flower despairingly. "I used to have this nice little café on the east side of town. It was a really popular place – too popular in fact because it started to get a lot of complaints from the law about things that were going on there."

"What kind of things?" Asked the princess.

"Noise, music, insurrection, all the usual sort of things," muttered One Flower vaguely.

"Insurrection?" Repeated Aurnia. "That means rebellion, right? People were using your café to plot rebellion against the sultan?"

"Rebellion, insurrection, those are really heavy terms," sighed the camelolean. "It's like I told

Captain Anders at the time; people liked to come to my café to relax, let their fur down and offload their problems. Sometimes those problems involved the sultan and the way things were run around here. The law started to take notice and come snooping around so I did what any responsible business owner would have done: borrowed money and paid them to go away. Only because word got around that soldiers were hanging around some of my customers didn't want to be seen around the place anymore. This meant I couldn't pay back the people I'd borrowed from and it also meant I couldn't pay off the soldiers who kept snooping around. So you see I was caught up in a vicious circle."

"A vicious circle entirely of your own making," scolded Aurnia.

"That's as the case may be, my sanctimonious princess friend, but once I was ensnared there was no way of escaping," sighed One Flower. "My creditors started closing in and the soldiers realised they weren't going to get their money and reported me directly to the sultan for trying to fan the flames of revolution. Before I knew it I was a wanted ungulate. I threw a rope over the city walls, climbed down into the desert and stole away into the night."

"And if it hadn't been for us you would have stayed free," sighed Aurnia sadly. "Well don't you worry, One Flower, I shall talk to the sultan and I'm sure we can come to some arrangement."

"I don't know about that," said One Flower fearfully. "The sultan is a pretty hot-tempered fellow. I'm worried I might really be for it this time."

"Hey!" Cried Captain Anders from behind. "No talking with the prisoner!"

Aurnia was forced to leave One Flower and re-joined her friends on the walk to the palace. As they walked they saw a young camelolean girl dressed in rags sweeping the street outside a shop. A fat man in colourful robes came out and began to shout at her. The cameolean hung her head in shame and began to cry.

"How awful," said Aurnia sympathetically. "What a way for a fellow to speak to their servant."

"Too right," replied Fenner. "I don't know how she puts up with it. If that were me I'd turn around and quit straight away."

"Maybe she can't afford to," said Fang. "She is not the only person I have seen around these streets dressed in rags. People in Firehara either seem to be very rich or very poor and the rich seem to be really hard on the poor."

"It looks like a harsh place to live despite its undeniable beauty," said Aurnia. "This hardly bodes well for our visit to the sultan."

"Leave it to me!" Said Goldenmane pompously. "The sultan is bound to be awed by my presence and with my unmatched skills in diplomacy it will not be long before he agrees to issue our common camelolean friend with a full and unconditional pardon."

Chapter Eight: The Sultan

The streets widened out and the houses became grander as Aurnia and her friends came within sight of the palace. The golden domes glittered so brightly it was hard to look at them directly whilst the arched windows were surprisingly small in comparison to the rest of the building, the walls built thick to keep out the heat.

Captain Anders came to a halt just before the palace gates. "Take the prisoner to the dungeons to await his fate," he instructed the four soldiers escorting One Flower. "I shall take the visitors to meet the sultan. He probably won't be too bothered to see most of them but the unicorn will doubtless be of great interest to him."

"Why of course," replied Goldenmane smugly.

Aurnia watched sadly as One Flower was hustled off around the side of the palace to the dungeon entrance. She was determined to help the camelolean so he would not suffer for his kindness to them and intended to raise his cause to the sultan at the first opportunity.

Captain Anders led the remaining friends through the palace gatehouse and through a lush green garden with palm trees and exotic plants growing all around. The garden was being tended by more servants in rags, their backs bent as they panted and sweated away in the intense heat whilst a well-dressed overseer with a big stick looked on. They waited whilst the captain exchanged a few words with the soldiers on duty who in turn looked up and smiled at Goldenmane. The unicorn was very pleased by the attention. "You see!" Said the unicorn happily. "They are overawed by me! It is only natural of course."

Captain Anders stood back as the large double doors of the palace were opened wide. Aurnia and her friends followed him inside. They found themselves in a very large and high room with a domed ceiling. The walls were brightly painted with colourful murals and the floor was covered in very thick carpets. There was a smell of spice and sweet perfume in the air.

The captain led them to a reception area near another set of doors. The reception area contained long red velvet settees and there were tapestries on the walls depicting scenes of epic battle in the desert. "Wait there," he instructed. "I shall go and announce your presence to the sultan."

The captain disappeared into the next room and was gone a long time. There was a large bowl of fruit on a low table to which the friends gladly helped themselves.

"This is delicious!" Exclaimed Fenner as he munched into a succulent apple. "I can't believe how dry my mouth got after so long walking out in the desert."

"Yes, the desert," muttered Goldenmane with a shudder as he helped himself to some grapes.

"I'm not relishing our return journey. Let's hope the sultan lets us stay here for a couple of days to refresh ourselves after the long journey."

Aurnia and her friends ate heartily of the fruit until it was all finished. "That's a shame," said Fenner as he stared down at the empty bowl. He looked up and saw a scaley walking past dressed in a servant's uniform (a scaley is a lizard-like creature with green skin that walks on two legs and has human-like hands and a long tail). "Hey!" Exclaimed the porcupine. "Any chance of some more fruit?"

The servant came hurrying over to Fenner and quickly snatched up the empty bowl. "Yes sir, right away sir!" He said fearfully. "Please don't tell the sultan I let the bowl get empty, sir!" The scaley hurried off only return a few moments later with the bowl filled with fruit once more. He set it down in front of them and retreated with a series of cowering bows.

"What a strange fellow," said Fenner as he watched the scaley go. "I mean I wasn't that scary, was I?"

"Strange indeed," muttered Fang suspiciously. "All the servants we see act very afraid."

"Probably just the culture around here," replied Goldenmane carelessly. "If you ask me, it can only be a good thing when common underlings act humbly towards their superiors. Of course, all of you lot are totally inferior to me and ought to be bowing down to me and obeying my every command just like that scaley fellow just now."

"Yet you're the one who carries me on your back," retorted Fenner as he helped himself to a banana. "Sounds pretty inferior to me. After all, aren't horses supposed to..."

"Enough!" Snapped Goldenmane crossly. "I don't need to listen to your ignorance when the sultan himself is about to receive me as his most honoured guest. Remember you are only here in the first place because of how noble I am. If I hadn't been here, you'd probably have been tossed into the dungeons with One Flower."

"Ah yes, One Flower," said Hector with a sad shake of his head. "We have to get him out of there. We owe it to him after all he's done for us."

"Yes, if it hadn't been for us, he'd have carried on living happily in his shack," agreed Lunar. "No matter what he might have done in the past I know he is a good creature at heart. We must persuade the sultan to show mercy."

Captain Anders came out of the door and snapped his fingers at the scaley servant. "You, over here!" He ordered harshly. The servant hurried over and bowed low. Captain Anders handed him a brush. "Smarten up that unicorn," he told him brusquely before turning to face the friends. "The sultan is almost ready to see you and is especially keen to meet the unicorn," he said.

"I expect he is!" Whinnied Goldenmane delightedly. "How pleasant it is to be appreciated by discerning company every now and again. It is no less than I deserve you know."

"Just don't let it go to your head," said Lunar.

"A little too late for that I think," muttered Fenner.

Captain Anders watched sternly as the frightened servant brushed Goldenmane's coat down with the brush to remove all the desert sand. As the servant worked, the captain barked orders and offered unconstructive criticism. Goldenmane, however, seemed delighted by the attention.

"Very well, that will have to do," muttered the captain. He snapped his fingers at the servant. "Depart!" He commanded.

"Very good sir, right away sir!" Simpered the servant as he turned and ran from the captain's presence.

Captain Anders looked the friends up and down and nodded. "Acceptable," he declared. "The sultan will see you now. Be sure to bow down low when you see him and remain respectful at all times."

The room into which Captain Anders led them was long and narrow with thick walls and small arched windows. There were deep carpets on the floor and plump cushions as big as chairs. On a raised platform, seated on a magnificent golden throne, was a very fat camelolean dressed in a long multicoloured robe. On either side of him stood two servants, dressed a little better than the others in clean white rags instead of brown sackcloth. The servants were holding huge feather fans which they were waving up and down to keep the sultan cool in the heat which seemed a little ridiculous to Aurnia because the sultan was, after all, a camelolean who thrived in this kind of heat.

The captain walked ahead of them and bowed down low. "The visitors here to see you, Your Excellency," he said reverently.

The sultan reclined on his throne and rubbed his chin thoughtfully, his eyes immediately affixing upon Goldenmane. Slowly he broke into a smile and beckoned them forward. "Captain Anders has told me but little about you," he said lazily. "My name is Sultan Lazlo Sandhoof the Second, supreme ruler of Firehara. Come closer, why don't you, and let me see what you are all about."

Aurnia came to the front of the party and bowed down low. "Honoured to meet you, Your Excellency," she said respectfully in the big voice her mother had taught her to use when addressing important people. "My name is Princess Aurnia of Cominaer. My friends and I are lost travellers desperately seeking a way home and..."

"Does it speak?" Interrupted the sultan suddenly.

Aurnia looked up in surprise. "I beg your pardon?" She said in confusion.

"The unicorn," stated the sultan simply. "Does it speak?"

"Indeed I do!" Replied Goldenmane arrogantly as he stepped forwards and came to stand right in front of the sultan's throne. "My name is Lord Goldenmane of the unicorn tribe. You are doubtless honoured to make my acquaintance."

The sultan raised his eyes in surprise. "Well, well," he said, clearly impressed. "This is even better than I expected. So you're a clever sort of creature then are you?"

"Some call me a genius, it is true," replied Goldenmane with pretend modesty. "Of course, it is not for me to say."

"Can you do tricks?" Asked the sultan.

"Tricks?" Repeated Goldenmane in confusion.

"Yes, you know, jump through hoops of fire or dance or sing or anything like that?" Said the sultan.

"Oh no, nothing like that," replied Goldenmane haughtily. "I mean dancing and jumping through hoops is all rather common don't you think, and singing is common too unless it is a song praising me and the unicorn tribe for being the noblest creatures created by the spirits of fate."

"I can sing and dance if you'd like," chirped up Fenner hopefully. "And I'd give jumping through a hoop of fire a go as well if there was a decent meal at the end of it."

"Be quiet, porcupine!" Snapped the sultan harshly. "I don't see what business you have talking in the first place seeing as you're nothing more than a wretched tundra animal."

"Oh quite right!" Exclaimed Goldenmane, nodding his head in agreement and snorting with laughter. "You know I've been stuck with this common creature on no less than four adventures and he never ceases to enrage me with his lowborn taunts and sneers. The sooner he shuts up the better, that's what I say!"

The sultan held up his hand for silence and looked at Aurnia and her friends in turn. "None of you are very interesting to me," he said at last. "None of you except the unicorn." He turned to Aurnia. "You are a princess, yes?"

"That's right," replied Aurnia. "Princess Aurnia of Cominaer, daughter of King Vriktor and Queen Ebetha."

"Never heard of them," snapped the sultan shortly. "And I've only vaguely heard of Cominaer too."

"But you have heard of it?" Said Aurnia keenly. "Might you know how we can get back there?"

"I don't know and I don't care," declared the sultan. "Still, somebody might be able to help you if you wander around long enough. Try the library; they're all pretty clever in there."

"Thank you, Your Excellency, we shall do that," replied Aurnia gratefully.

"But anyway, let's get down to business," said the sultan. "You are the princess so I take it you own this unicorn?"

"Own me?" Cried Goldenmane in astonishment. "Nobody could possibly 'own' the noble Lord Goldenmane. Why is anything it should be me who..."

"Princess Aurnia is Lord Goldenmane's liege," said Lunar helpfully, interrupting before Goldenmane's arrogance ended up offending the sultan. "Back home in Cominaer he served as the ambassador from the unicorn tribe but the king also gave him the task of carrying the princess's baggage during her many adventures."

"Ah, so like a pack pony huh?" Muttered the sultan thoughtfully as he inclined his hand towards Goldenmane. "Do you not think that a little disrespectful? Treating a magnificent creature like this as a common horse?"

"Well exactly!" Exclaimed Goldenmane dramatically. "And you cannot even begin to imagine the other indignities I have been put through. Take this porcupine for instance. All day long he taunts and mocks me and nobody says a word to him."

The sultan tutted and shook his head. "This will not do," he declared. "This will not do at all." He looked at Aurnia again. "Very well, I shall give you five hundred gold pieces."

Aurnia's mouth dropped open in astonishment. "Oh," she said. "Well thank you very much, Your Excellency. That's certainly most generous, but I don't quite understand."

"What is there not to understand?" demanded the Sultan. "I am going to give you five hundred gold pieces, free use of my library to help you find your way home and all the food you can eat at the finest restaurant in the city. Do you accept or not?"

"Oh, well…" began Aurnia.

"Yes!" Exclaimed Fenner excitedly. "Yes, we do! Gold, the library and food – especially the food!"

"Excellent, we have a deal," said the sultan smugly. "Captain Anders will take care of everything you need and I shall even throw in a little bonus because I'm feeling so generous." He snapped his fingers. The scaley servant who had found them another bowl of fruit and brushed down Goldenmane came scurrying into the room and fell face down on the floor in front of the Sultan. "You called, Your Excellency?" Squeaked the scaley fearfully.

"Indeed so," replied the sultan regally. "You see these folks here? I am giving them leave to remain in the city for the next five days. I want you to go with them and cater to their every whim. If you fail me or I hear they are dissatisfied I shall throw you into the deepest pit of the dungeon and you will remain there forever, do you understand?"

"Yes, Your Excellency!" Replied the scaley fearfully. He looked up at Aurnia. "Delighted to make your acquaintance, ma'am," he muttered although he seemed anything but delighted.

"Well I don't quite know what to say," muttered Aurnia.

"Yes, it is quite unexpected," agreed Lunar.

The sultan yawned and stretched out his arms. "Well anyway, I am tired and it is almost time for my nap," he declared lazily. "The slaves will show you out."

"I'm sorry, what?" Said Fenner in surprise.

The sultan ignored him and turned to Captain Anders. "Take the unicorn and see him fitted out in my livery colours," he instructed. "See if you can teach him some tricks whilst you're at it so he can better entertain my guests. His pompous outbursts are quite funny for now but I'm worried they'll get boring after a while."

"Yes, Your Excellency," said Captain Anders respectfully. He stepped forwards and tossed a rein and bit over Goldenmane's head. "Alright then, unicorn, giddy-up."

"What?" Cried Goldenmane in astonishment. "What is the meaning of this?"

"The purchase has been completed," said the sultan flatly. "This unicorn is my slave now."

"What? No!" Cried Aurnia in horror. "We never agreed to any such thing!"

"Oh but you did," retorted the sultan. "Or rather your porcupine representative agreed to it."

"Hey, I know Lord Goldenmane and I have had our differences but I would never want him to be sold as a slave!" Said Fenner. "I didn't even know you had slaves here in Firehara!"

"Well of course we have slaves," replied Captain Anders flatly. "You didn't think we'd keep servants around who we had to pay, did you?"

"But we never agreed to any such thing!" Said Aurnia. "We would never sell Lord Goldenmane to anyone; he isn't even mine to sell!"

"You are his liege are you not?" Asked the sultan reasonably.

"I suppose so, in a manner of speaking," replied Aurnia. "But..."

"The Unicorn Council will not stand for this!" Shouted Goldenmane as Captain Anders tugged at his bridle to lead him away. "You cannot enslave one who is of the superior tribe of unicorns, it is an outrage against the spirits of fate!"

"If the Unicorn Council wants to object one of them can come and stand before me in person and do it themselves," retorted the sultan. "Then I will enslave them as well and have two unicorns." He chuckled. "But I don't think there is much to worry about on that score. A unicorn hasn't been seen around these parts for hundreds of years and as you say, you are lost and far from home." He turned to Aurnia and her remaining friends. "Now then, my steward will be waiting for you outside to give you your five hundred pieces of gold."

"But we'd rather have Goldenmane!" Persisted Aurnia. "This isn't fair; you've tricked us!"

"The deal was done fair and square," snapped the sultan regally. "And I am in charge here. If you continue to complain I shall have you buried feet first in the desert sand until only your heads are visible. How would you like that, huh?"

"This is all that stupid porcupine's fault!" Cried Goldenmane as the captain and his soldiers came to drag him away.

"For once I'm in full agreement!" Wailed Fenner despairingly. "I really am a stupid porcupine to have fallen for such a cheap trick."

At that moment Guselin leapt out of the knapsack pocket and landed on the carpet in front of the sultan's throne. "Aha!" Laughed the frog triumphantly. "So the unicorn has become ensnared in my trap, huh? Ah yes, it is all part of my plan; there is no getting away you know!"

The sultan looked at the frog in surprise. "And who might you be?" He demanded haughtily.

"My name is Guselin the Mighty!" Boasted the frog as he hopped up and down excitedly. "Guselin the Great, Guselin the Invincible, Guselin the..."

"Guselin the pet," said Aurnia quickly, anxious not to cause yet more trouble. "This is nobody of any significance at all, Your Excellency, it is just my idiot pet."

"The princess lies!" Snapped Guselin angrily. "There is none who can match my power or defy me! Oh no! It is all part of my plan! Aha!"

The sultan smiled. "What an amusing little creature," he remarked. "I shall give you five gold pieces for him."

"The favour of the mighty Guselin cannot be purchased with mere coin!" Declared Guselin arrogantly. "And besides, I am not interested in your coin. I am interested in your doom! Aha!"

"All in all I think this has been a most profitable exchange for both parties," said the sultan smugly. "Now then, I think that's enough purchases for today. I am tired and am needing a nap."

"A creature after my own heart, huh?" Declared Guselin. "Aha! Yes! I see the two of us are going to get along just fine. Together we shall rule over all; I as the supreme leader and you as my dutiful underling. It is just as I envisaged it would be. Oh yes!"

"You're going to be a slave just like Lord Goldenmane you silly frog," said Lunar crossly.

"Aha! That's where you're wrong!" Countered Guselin. "The sultan wishes for me to rule alongside him!"

"No actually the wolf is quite right," said the sultan as one of his slaves came forwards and scooped Guselin up into a large glass jar. "You're going to be a slave."

"Aha! Yes! Comrade! Equal! Partner!" Laughed Guselin obliviously as he hopped delightedly around the circular confines of his new prison.

Chapter Nine: The Streets of Firehara

Aurnia and her friends desperately argued their case but the sultan was in no mood to listen. Instead, he declared he was tired and had them ushered out of the room. A nervous steward approached them in the waiting area and handed them a big bag of coins before ushering them back along the corridor and out through the large front doors. Before they knew it they were back on the street once more.

"I cannot believe this is happening!" Groaned Aurnia. "The sultan completely outplayed us and now both Goldenmane and Guselin are his slaves."

"And we didn't even get to ask about One Flower," sighed Fang. "We have some big problems, all right."

"But hey, at least we're not paupers," said Fenner, motioning towards the bag of coins. "I wonder how much five hundred gold pieces gets you around here anyway."

"Yes, it was generous of the sultan to give us the money at least," said Hector. "Hey, maybe he's not all bad after all."

"People who are that rich don't know the meaning of money," replied Fang. "It was a cruel trick he played on us and we have to do something about it. We have to think of a way to get Goldenmane and Guselin back – and we have to get One Flower out of prison too."

"I don't know about Guselin, he seemed quite happy where he was," said Fenner.

"As we all know from experience, Guselin is entertaining at first but soon he just becomes annoying," said Aurnia. "The sultan will get bored of him and who knows what he will do? He will probably throw him into the dungeons with One Flower." She looked around the crowded streets of this strange city before them. "What a muddle," she sighed despondently. "Where do we even begin?"

There came a nervous coughing from behind them. Aurnia turned around to see the elderly scaley slave standing before them, wringing his hands nervously. "Begging your pardon, Your Highness," said the scaley in a meek voice. "But the sultan has assigned me to your service. I hope my assistance proves satisfactory."

"Oh goodness, of course," said Aurnia pleasantly. "In all the excitement I quite forgot. The sultan said you were to help us find our way around the city, didn't he?"

"That's right, Your Highness," replied the scaley. "My name is Shuffler and I am here to help in any way I can."

"Well, you can start by taking us to this restaurant!" Exclaimed Fenner. "The sultan said it would be free, right? And that we could have as much as we can eat?"

"Fenner!" Exclaimed Lunar. "How can you think of food at a time like this?"

"Hey, I want to rescue our friends as much as you but I can't think on an empty stomach," replied the porcupine with a shrug.

Shuffler led the friends down the main street and into a large square where a busy and colourful bazaar was in full swing. Traders were selling spices from large urns and huge carpets were strung over pieces of string and hung up like washing. There was silk and exotic clothes and precious ornaments and jewellery, each sold from an individual uncovered stall. Some of the items being sold were so valuable they needed to be guarded by burly bodyguards who stood on either side of the stall with their arms folded. Meanwhile the traders advertised their wares by holding the up over their heads and shouting at the tops of their voices. "It looks like there are traders from all over the world selling their stuff here," said Lunar. "Perhaps one of them has heard of Cominaer and can tell us how to get back."

"Yes, this bazaar is definitely worth exploring when we have time," agreed Aurnia. She turned to look at Shuffler. "You don't mind showing us around later do you, Shuffler?"

"Oh no, Your Highness, not in the least," simpered the scaley. "Anything I can do to help, Your Highness, anything at all."

"You know you can call me Aurnia," said Aurnia pleasantly.

"Oh no, Your Highness, I had better not," replied Shuffler. "It is very disrespectful, Your Highness."

"Only you are being rather meek and to be honest it is already quite annoying and we've only just met," said Aurnia. "I'm not sure I can take much more of it."

Shuffler cringed and bowed down so low his nose almost touched the floor. "I'm so sorry, Your Highness, it seems I have displeased you already! Please take pity on an old man, Your Highness, I am trying my best!"

"You don't need to be humble around us, Shuffler," said Lunar kindly. "We all think keeping creatures as slaves is a horrible thing to do."

"That's very kind, Your Wolfness," said Shuffler. "But the fact of the matter is slavery is a thing here in Firehara and I just have to accept it. There is nothing I can do. If I don't serve you as I am supposed to the sultan will throw me into the dungeons."

"This sultan really is a nasty piece of work," snapped Aurnia. "I have to say he makes me very cross indeed."

"Well here we are," said Shuffler as he stopped outside a tall flat roofed building with an awning covering the frontage. "The finest place to eat in all of Firehara. Or so I'm told. I've never been allowed to eat here of course."

"Well that's going to change today," said Aurnia decisively. "You're going to come with us and enjoy a fine meal the same as the rest of us. After all, you're part of the gang now."

The inside of the restaurant was dark and smoky. At the back of the room a band of slaves was playing lute and pipe music and there was an almost overwhelming scent of spices which pervaded throughout. A waiter hurried forwards and bowed down low as the friends came in. "The princess and her friends," said the waiter humbly. "The sultan's men said you would be coming. Please, come this way."

The waiter led the way to a back room which was clearly reserved for only the most important visitors because everybody else dining there was dressed in expensive clothes and was clearly very rich. He seated the friends at a long table with a multicoloured tablecloth and snapped his fingers. Immediately a group of five slaves came out carrying huge silver trays on their shoulders which they set down on the table in front of the party. On the trays was every time of exotic food imaginable. There were toffee fruits, spiced mushrooms, salted pears, sugared almonds, five different types of rice, hard and soft cheese and vegetable curries both hot and sweet.

"Wow!" Cried Fenner as he began to greedily shovel food on to his plate. "Now this I what I call a feast!"

The food was indeed delicious and the friends ate hungrily, for they had not had a proper hot meal since they had arrived at One Flower's shack a few days before.

"Are you going to have some, Shuffler?" Asked Aurnia as she helped herself to some more sweet curry and rice.

"Oh no, I don't think I ought to, Your Highness," replied the scaley slave meekly.

"Oh come on!" Urged Fenner. "Think of us as friends. Don't tell me you're not hungry?"

"Oh, well that's very kind of you, Your Prickliness," replied Shuffler and with that he reached forwards, helped himself to a single lettuce leaf and started to nervously nibble like a rabbit.

"He's a bit of a strange fellow isn't he?" Whispered Lunar to Aurnia.

The princess nodded. "I'm sure it isn't his fault though," she said. "He's probably been tormented so long by the sultan he doesn't know how to assert himself."

"I wish there was something we could do to help him," said the young wolf.

Aurnia thought for a moment. "Perhaps there is," she said, looking down at the purse full of coins that was hanging heavily on her belt. She turned to Shuffler. "How much does a slave cost around here?" She asked him.

Shuffler looked at the princess in alarm. "Surely you are not thinking of purchasing another slave!" He said in alarm. "Oh woe! I have failed you! I am so useless and the sultan is going to be so angry!"

"Not at all, don't be silly," replied Aurnia firmly. "I was just thinking that if Goldenmane was worth five hundred gold pieces how much would a scaley slave be worth?"

"Oh not much at all, Your Highness," sighed Shuffler sadly. "We scaleys aren't very highly sought after I am afraid. You could probably pick up an average scaley slave for about one hundred gold pieces."

"Excellent!" Exclaimed Aurnia happily. "Then it is settled!"

"What's settled?" Asked Lunar.

"Just you wait and see," replied the princess as she finished up the last of her curry. "Come on everyone, we are going back to the sultan's palace!"

Chapter Ten: One Flower In The Dungeons

"The sultan accepts your offer," said the steward formally as he and Aurnia stood in the reception area of the palace. Aurnia thanked him and counted out one hundred gold pieces which the steward then placed into a chest and locked up. Aurnia went back outside to her friends, a broad smile upon her face as she addressed Shuffler. "It is all done," she told him. "I have paid one hundred gold pieces to the sultan. You are free to go."

"I don't understand, Your Highness," said Shuffler in confusion.

"You heard me," smiled Aurnia. "The sultan agreed to sell you to me for one hundred gold pieces. I paid that money to free you. You are no longer a slave."

"Really?" Replied Shuffler, standing up a little straighter and looking at Aurnia with a new light in his eyes. "You paid the sultan so I don't have to be a slave anymore?"

"That's right," said the princess. "And also I am going to give you fifty gold pieces to help you get back on your feet as a free man." She handed Shuffler a small purse containing the coin.

"So you're giving me fifty gold pieces and I'm a free man?" Said Shuffler.

"That's right," replied Aurnia. "So now there's no need for you to bow down to us or anyone else. We can come together as equals and find a way to rescue our friends from the clutches of this wicked sultan!"

"Oh no, I don't think so," replied Shuffler. His voice had changed and he sounded far more confident now.

"What do you mean?" Asked Aurnia.

"Well it is like you just said, there is no need for me to bow down to you or anyone else," replied the scaley. "So you can get lost. Why should I help you rescue your friends? I don't know them and I don't care about them either. That unicorn in particular seemed especially annoying. I'm glad he's a slave."

"But Princess Aurnia just paid for your freedom out of her own money!" Cried Hector indignantly. "Surely you cannot be so ungrateful?"

"She didn't have to," said Shuffler with a shrug. "And besides, I've been a slave for over twenty-five years. It is time for me to start living. I'm going straight back to that restaurant to stuff my face with the finest food they have to offer." And with that he pushed past Aurnia and her friends and began to strut off in the direction of the bazaar with his head held high. Along the way he bumped into a slave carrying a stack of wooden boxes in his hands. "Get out of the way you stupid worthless slave!" Spat Shuffler furiously and with that he kicked the slave in the shin, sending him staggering backwards and unbalancing the boxes so that they all tipped over and broke against the cobblestones. The slave's master came hurrying out of his shop and began to hit the slave with a stout wooden stick as he scolded him about the boxes. Shuffler folded his arms and laughed heartily at the slave's misfortune before carrying on his way.

"But wait!" Cried Aurnia as she hurried after the scaley. "You're the only one who knows his way around the city; we're complete strangers here!"

"Too bad, you little squirt!" Chuckled Shuffler as he rudely barged past another wretched slave. "You should have thought about that before you freed me. Do you know how hard it has been to hold my tongue and act humble over the last twenty-five years? Well no longer! Now I'm really going to enjoy myself and say what I think, and what I think is that you can go and soak your head if you think I'm going to follow you around on some stupid adventure to rescue your idiot friends."

"What an ungrateful person you are!" Said Lunar angrily. "Can't you do anything to help us?"

"No I shall not!" Snapped the scaley rudely. "Nobody is going to tell me what to do ever again, especially not some stupid wolf."

Aurnia and her friends watched as Shuffler barged his way through the crowds towards the bazaar. "I know he was annoying when he was a slave," said the princess. "But I much preferred him to the brash and arrogant fellow he became as soon as he was freed. Still, I do not regret that we did it. Even though the situation has not turned out as we hoped it is still better to do the right thing, and the right thing was paying the sultan to free him. That doesn't sound too sanctimonious does it Lunar?"

"Perhaps a little," replied the young wolf. "But you're quite right all the same."

With Shuffler having so rudely departed, Aurnia and her friends stood aimlessly in the street wondering what to do.

"Perhaps we could go back to the sultan and ask him for help?" Suggested Fenner.

"We can hardly ask for help from our enemy," replied Fang reasonably. "After all, sooner or later we are going to have to confront him to rescue Goldenmane and Guselin."

"What about One Flower then?" Said Lunar. "We could go to the dungeons and see if there is anything we can do for him."

Fang nodded. "That's a good idea," he said. "After all, we still have some money left. Perhaps if our camelolean friend owes a fine we could pay it back for him with the money the sultan gave us."

The friends made their way back to the area around the castle and followed the narrow street down which they had seen the guards leading One Flower earlier. The city prison was a grey square building at the end of the street which appeared rather neglected. Scrubby grass was growing the yard and the walls were cracked in places but it appeared secure and well-guarded with bars covering the narrow windows and a single iron door guarded by a stone faced camelolean sentry.

As Aurnia approached, the sentry he glared at her and placed his hand on his sabre sword. "What do you want, girl?" He demanded sternly.

"I wish to see one of your prisoners," replied Aurnia with her big voice. "A Mr One Flower to be precise. I understand he was arrested earlier today."

The camelolean bared his yellow teeth in a mean grin. "We don't exactly have visiting times here, brat," he sneered. "It isn't that sort of jail."

"But we really need to see our friend," persisted Aurnia. "Look, we have some gold with us and thought we might be able to pay a fine if that is what it takes."

The sentry's expression changed. He looked eager and curious. "Gold you say? How much?"

"One hundred gold pieces," replied Aurnia, thinking quickly. "Is that enough?"

The sentry considered for a moment. "I will have to check," he said at last. He disappeared into the prison before returning a moment later and beckoning them inside. "This way please."

Aurnia and her friends were led into the main part of the jail. Even behind the thick walls the heat was oppressive.

"I wouldn't like to be a prisoner here," shuddered Fenner as he looked warily at the narrow slit windows set high up in the stone.

"I wouldn't like to be a prisoner anywhere," sighed Lunar. "Oh, to be back in the forests of Cominaer again."

The sentry stopped at a strong wooden desk. "Wait here," he instructed before vanishing off down a dark corridor, locking the door behind him. After a while he returned with another sentry walking alongside him. The second sentry marched straight up to Aurnia. "Let me see the money," he demanded promptly.

Aurnia reached for the purse and counted out the gold. The two guards snatched it up greedily and shared it between them. "That will do," said the first sentry. "I think you and the prisoner have some business to discuss. Follow me."

The two sentries led the way down the long dark corridor. "We seem to be running out of gold at an alarming rate," said Lunar worriedly.

"Yes, we should try and save some if we can," agreed Fang. "We don't know how much longer we're going to be here."

"One hundred gold pieces seems like a lot of money," said Hector thoughtfully. "I'd have been happy with ten."

"Its too late to haggle now," replied Aurnia. "I've already given them the money. And besides, one hundred gold pieces isn't a lot of money to me because I'm a princess."

"You're starting to sound like Goldenmane," teased Fenner.

"Well I only wish we hadn't wasted a penny on that ungrateful Shuffler," put in Lunar ruefully.

The sentries led them into the main cell block with heavy iron doors on either side. Here and there Aurnia could hear moaning coming from inside the cells and she felt very sorry for whoever was inside. the sentries led them to a cell at the far end and unlocked the door. From within the cell there came a mournful singing. Aurnia recognised the voice straight away. It was One Flower.

Oh Sultan friend!

I just don't understand

How you could keep me

Locked up below ground

Don't you know

That's just not cool, man?

I just want to go home

To my shack in the sands

I'm a lonely – camelolean!

Yes a lonely – camelolean!

Just a lonely – camelolean!

I'm a lonely - camelolean!

Hey sultan friend – peace

Its just not fair

Why won't you release me

Into the cool fresh air?

Don't keep me down here

Trapped in this lair

Hear my cries, brother

Don't be such a square!

I'm a lonely – camelolean!

Yes a lonely – camelolean!

Just a lonely – camelolean!

I'm a lonely - camelolean!

"Here you go," said the first sentry briskly. "You can have five minutes."

"Five minutes?" Repeated Fenner indignantly. "Hey, that's hardly value for money you know. A hundred gold pieces for five minutes? That's twenty gold pieces per minute – basically one gold piece every three seconds!"

"That's some impressive maths skills you've got there, Fenner," smiled Lunar. "Did you ever consider a career as Aurnia's tutor?"

"Enough!" Snapped the second guard crossly. "You have five minutes. If you don't like it you can just clear out with nothing."

"Five minutes will be fine," said Fang quickly before Fenner could argue further. He led the way inside the cramped cell with the others following. The guard closed and locked the door behind them. One Flower was lying on an uncomfortable hammock just below the barred window. He looked up as they came in and smiled weakly. "Hey there princess and animal friends," he said in surprise. "Good of you to come and see me."

"Goodness me what a pickle you are in," sighed Aurnia as she looked around the bare cell. "Why didn't you say it was the sultan himself you had upset? We wouldn't have pressured you to guide us."

"Oh you know, I didn't want to worry you," replied One Flower with a shrug.

"We went to the sultan and tried to ask for his mercy but he said no," said Fenner.

"You've met the sultan?" Replied the camelolean in surprise.

"Indeed we did, and he ended up taking Goldenmane and Guselin as his slaves," said Lunar.

"Oh he's a real sneaky guy that sultan," sighed One Flower with a sad shake of his head. "Why didn't I warn you about him before? We might all have saved ourselves a lot of bother!"

"Well regardless of what the sultan said we are going to help you," said Aurnia.

"That's a kind thought, princess friend, but I'm afraid it is quite hopeless," sighed One Flower. "There is nothing that can be done – you certainly can't break through these thick stone walls and tomorrow I am to be sent to the mines."

"The mines?" Repeated Fang.

"Yes, the salt mines just to the west of here," replied One Flower. "All the prisoners end up there eventually, toiling as slaves in the narrow tunnels until they collapse from exhaustion!"

"But you don't deserve to be sent to the salt mines!" Exclaimed Aurnia indignantly. "You didn't even do that much wrong; from what I can gather you were only running your café. You didn't even mean the sultan harm in the first place."

"Sadly the sultan doesn't see it that way," shrugged the camelolean. "He hates anyone who crosses him – even if they only cross him in a small way."

"Something has to be done," declared Fang gravely. "We cannot allow this wicked sultan to tyrannise his own people like this." The older wolf cast his eyes around the cell. Aurnia knew well what he was thinking. He was trying to figure out a means of escape and yet as Aurnia saw it there was none. The dungeons were secure and well-guarded, the thick walls quite impregnable.

The door unlocked and the sentry appeared. "Times up," said the sentry abruptly. "Time to leave before somebody important comes along and finds you here."

"Hey!" Exclaimed Fenner indignantly. "That was never five minutes!"

"Too bad," snapped the sentry. "You either leave now or you stay here and get sent to the mines in the morning."

There was nothing for it. The friends bade One Flower a reluctant goodbye and followed the sentry back through the corridor and out of the door.

Chapter Eleven: A Cheap Trick

"This is awful," groaned Hector despairingly. "Nothing is going right for us."

"At least we still have some gold," said Fenner optimistically.

"Gold?" Came a voice from behind them. "Did I hear mention of gold?"

Aurnia and her friends turned around. Before them stood a very tall and fat camelolean dressed in garish and very expensive looking multicoloured robes.

"What do you want?" Demanded Fenner rudely.

"What do I want? Why I want to help you stay rich of course," replied the camelolean smoothly. "Or rather I want to help you become even richer. I can help you double your riches with this ingenious contraption I have just invented."

The camelolean snapped his fingers. A skinny scaley came hurrying out of a tall tent and handed him a stout wooden box with a velvet curtain across the front. "Gather round," said the camelolean mysteriously. "Let me demonstrate my wonderous creation."

Aurnia and Lunar looked at one another sceptically but there was something hypnotic about the way the camelolean spoke and so they came closer and watched carefully as he held the strange little box aloft before them. The scaley servant hovered around them, pointing and clapping enthusiastically in a way they all found to be highly annoying.

"Now then," began the camelolean with a flourish. "This appears to be an ordinary box with a curtain attached to it, does it not?"

"Look! Look!" Cried the scaley assistant excitedly.

"We can see perfectly well thank you," snapped Aurnia crossly. "Please stop jostling us and let us see."

The camelolean drew back the curtain on the box to reveal the inside, which was empty. "Now then!" He exclaimed. "Look at this."

The camelolean took from his pocket a gold coin and placed it within the box before closing the curtain. He shook the box above his head, lowered it and opened the curtain once more. Inside were two gold coins. "Behold!" He exclaimed. "I have invented a magical box which doubles your money! You don't even have to learn a spell."

"Wow!" Exclaimed Hector in wonder. "That's some magic!"

"Magic my paw!" Exclaimed Fang crossly. "I've seen that trick done a thousand times at village fairs back home in Cominaer. You are nothing more than a cheap trickster!"

"I'll have you know I am an honest and upstanding tradesman," snapped the camelolean indignantly. "My magical money doubling box is totally genuine and legit!"

"What a waste of our time," sighed Aurnia as she turned to leave.

"Guess there's one born every minute," muttered Fenner with a wry shake of his head.

"Let's just get out of here," said Lunar. "What annoying people you meet in Firhara."

The friends turned and walked away, ignoring the camelolean's protests behind them. They walked around a corner and joined the busy main street. It was dusk and the market traders were packing up for the day. "What shall we do now?" Asked Aurnia.

"We should find a place to sleep for the night," replied Fang. "I get the feeling these streets won't be safe after dark."

"We should get some food too," added Fenner. "At least we still have lots of gold left. We should be able to find somewhere good."

Aurnia yawned and stretched. "I'm exhausted," she declared. "A fine inn with good food and a warm feather bed is exactly what I need. I know we need to save money but we have been through so much today that I'm sure it will be ok to treat ourselves just once."

Aurnia reached for her purse but to her horror it was not there. She looked down and saw that it had been cut at the strings around her belt. She gasped in horror. "The purse with the gold coins inside!" She cried. "What has happened to it?"

"Oh no!" Cried Fenner. "This can't be happening."

"Where could it have gone?" Asked Hector. "When did you last have it?"

"I definitely had it when I left the jail," replied Aurnia as she thought hard.

"The camelolean and the scaley!" Exclaimed Lunar. "It can only have been them! That conjuring trick was just a distraction whilst the assistant stole the purse. Oh no, why didn't we see this coming?"

"That must have been why the scaley was jostling us," groaned Fenner.

"Quickly!" Urged Fang as he started to run. "Let's get back there and challenge them!"

Led by the wolves, the friends hurried back around the corner to confront the camelolean and his assistant but it was no use. The street was deserted, the deceivers long gone.

"What are we going to do now?" Cried Fenner. "This city is huge; we will never find them!"

"Are we totally out of money?" Asked Lunar.

"Yes I'm afraid so," replied Aurnia quietly.

"So we don't have anywhere to sleep tonight?" Asked Hector.

"So we don't have anything to *eat* tonight?" Added Fenner.

"I'm so sorry everyone," sighed Aurnia. She blamed herself for what had happened and felt very bad.

"Now then it will not be so bad," said Fang, thinking fast. "We have slept outside before in the forests, remember, and myself and Lunar will keep guard through the night. As for food, there must be something in your knapsack, Aurnia."

"Perhaps a few salted biscuits," replied the princess.

"Well there you go, that's better than nothing," said the older wolf.

"Not for a growing porcupine like myself," muttered Fenner. "And to sleep outside too?"

"A common porcupine like you ought to be used to sleeping outside," said Lunar, imitating Goldenmane. Everyone laughed despite the seriousness of their situation.

"Yes, I suppose Lord Goldenmane and Guselin do have it worse," acknowledged Aurnia. "At least we're still free."

"At least they get to sleep under a roof tonight," replied Fenner.

Night descended quickly. The friends wandered the streets in the dark looking for a comfortable place to sleep. Fang kept to the front of the party, Lunar behind, protecting the friends against potential dangers lurking in the shadows. Fang led them down a wide alley where they found a deeply arched stone doorway which seemed to be part of a warehouse. "Here," he said as he came to a halt and sniffed the air. "This looks like as good a place as any."

Aurnia and her friends settled down in the doorway as best they could with the wolves taking it in turns to stand guard against danger. At night in the city, as in the desert, it got very cold and Aurnia shivered as she tried to get comfortable in her blanket. She reflected ruefully upon their bad luck and the horrible people they had encountered ever since they had arrived here in Firehara. What was even worse they had been delayed and now seemed further than ever from finding their way back home to Cominaer and her parents.

Chapter Twelve: Yet Another Betrayal

Aurnia woke up a little before dawn. It was still very cold and her muscles ached from lying on the hard floor. Lunar was standing guard just beyond the archway. Aurnia got up and went to join her.

"I wonder what the day will bring?" Said the princess as she watched the first embers of the sun appear on the horizon.

"More danger and adventure I'll be bound," replied the young wolf with a shudder.

Aurnia patted Lunar reassuringly. Her friend was prone to worrying, especially when outside of her natural forest habitat.

"I have no idea what we are going to do," sighed Lunar. "Goldenmane and Guselin are slaves, all of our money has been pinched and we can't leave One Flower behind either considering we're sort of to blame for getting him arrested and thrown into prison. I'm sorry, Lunar, but I don't have the first clue how we're going to get ourselves out of this one."

Fenner got up and came to join them. "Good morning," he said cheerily. "What's for breakfast?"

Aurnia went and looked in her knapsack as Hector and Fang rose from their sleep. "Just a few pieces of stale bread I'm afraid," she told them sorrowfully.

"A growing porcupine cannot live on bread alone but I suppose it is better than nothing," sighed Fenner.

The friends ate sadly as they watched the sun come up. Soon the cold was gone and it was unbearably hot once more.

"So what *are* we going to do?" Asked Lunar.

"Let's go back to the main street and see if we can catch sight of the rogues who robbed us yesterday," replied Fang. "It might take a while to find them but without money there isn't a thing we can do in this city."

Aurnia and her friends left the archway and made their way back to the city's main thoroughfare. The market traders were unpacking their stalls and advertising their wares and although the princess scanned the faces of the crowd she could see no sign of the fiendish camelolean and his thieving scaley assistant.

As Aurnia and her friends were stood on the pavement watching the people go past the princess spied a familiar face. Shuffler was jauntily making his way down the middle of the street swinging his arms carelessly and whistling a tune. He looked up and saw the friends and came over. "Oh hello," he said cheerily.

"What do you want?" Demanded Fenner crossly. "I can't believe you have the nerve to talk to us."

"Yes, get out of here you ungrateful wretch," growled Lunar.

"That's not a very nice welcome to give a friend," said Shuffler, pretending to sound hurt.

"Some friend you turned out to be," said Hector accusingly.

Shuffler folded his arms and looked at them closely. "You all look awful," he said critically. "Like you spent the night sleeping outside or something."

"Thanks," muttered Aurnia icily. "Now go away."

"Why are you up so early anyway?" Asked Shuffler, not at all bothered by their contempt. "I would have thought you would have been living the good life at the best tavern in town with all that money the sultan gave you."

"If you must know we have indeed spent the night on the streets," snapped Aurnia irritably. "You're quite a perceptive fellow, do you know that?"

"Yes, we were conned out of all our money and robbed," added Lunar sadly. "But for all that you're still the worst person we've met here."

"Conned and robbed huh?" Replied Shuffler. He threw back his head and laughed. "Ha! That's really funny. You stupid idiots!"

"Yes, laugh at our misfortune why don't you?" Snapped Fenner crossly.

"I shall," taunted Shuffler.

"Oh just go away will you?" Cried Aurnia furiously. "You really are one of the worst creatures I have ever met in my life and when you consider some of the people I've met on my adventures that's actually quite an achievement!"

Shuffler stopped laughing and considered for a moment. "Hey, now I come to think of it maybe I have been a little ungrateful," he said.

"A little?" Replied Lunar.

"Perhaps I can help you," said the scaley thoughtfully.

"Help us? Help us how?" Asked Fang.

"I have friends in high places you know," replied Shuffler mysteriously. "All those years as a slave to the sultan saw me meeting some of the most important people in the city. Now that I'm free I'm sure they'll be only too happy to help me."

"I'm not sure they'll give you the time of day," said Lunar sceptically.

"Be that as it may you want to be back with your friends don't you?" Said Shuffler reasonably. "That unicorn and the camelolean you came here with?"

"Why of course," replied Fang.

"Well in that case I know just the man to help," smiled Shuffler.

Aurnia and her friends looked at one another. "You owe us big do you know that?" Snapped

Fenner. "You owe us for freeing you and for being so ungrateful."

"And I intend to repay you," replied Shuffler smoothly.

"Very well, let's go and meet this friend of yours," said Fang.

Aurnia and the rest of the party followed the scaley through the busy streets. "I have been thinking about the way I behaved yesterday and I realise I was very ungrateful," said Shuffler. "I am glad I saw you so that I might make it up to you."

"We forgive you," replied Aurnia graciously. "It must have been very upsetting being a slave for so long."

"Oh believe me it was," replied Shuffler with a shudder.

Shuffler led them to a tall domed building just beyond the prison and asked them to wait for him outside.

"What is this place?" Asked Lunar.

"This is where my friend works," replied Shuffler.

"And what does your friend do?" Asked Fang.

"Actually I think you have already met him," smirked Shuffler. "His name is Captain Anders

"Ah, I see now," said Hector. "You're going to report the theft of our gold so that all the guards will be keeping an eye out for the culprits."

"Yes, yes I'm going to tell the captain all about your misfortune," replied Shuffler smoothly. "Now wait here."

Shuffler vanished into the domed building. The friends waited impatiently outside. "I could have reported the crime myself," muttered Aurnia. "Still, I suppose we shouldn't be ungrateful. It does seem as though Shuffler genuinely wants to make it up to us."

"Well I have a bad feeling," said Fenner. "I don't like that we have to trust that slippery creature."

"It looks like you're right!" Exclaimed Lunar in alarm. "Watch out everyone!"

Before Aurnia or her friends could react a group of guards with their swords drawn rushed out of the building and surrounded them. Shuffler hurried behind them. "That's them, captain!" He exclaimed maliciously. "That's the vagrants!

"Vagrants?" Repeated Aurnia in horror. "What are you talking about? We haven't done a thing!"

Captain Anders stepped forwards to face them. "Ah yes, I recognise this sorry rabble from yesterday," he said sternly.

"Sir, you have to help us," urged Hector. "We're not the criminals, we're the victims! All our money has been stolen and we don't have a penny to our name."

The captain rubbed his chin thoughtfully. "So you are flat broke, huh?"

"Yes sir," replied Fenner. "We don't have a bean."

"Well," announced Captain Anders officiously. "It would appear as though a very serious crime has been committed."

Lunar breathed a sigh of relief. "Thank goodness you've seen sense!" She exclaimed. "For a moment there I thought…"

"A serious crime has been committed *by you all*!" Interrupted the captain harshly.

Aurnia and her friends gasped. "What do you mean?" Demanded the princess.

"Vagrancy is a very serious offence here in Firehara," said Anders. "The sultan doesn't like beggars and layabouts."

"But we're neither of those things," protested Lunar. "We were robbed, it wasn't out fault."

"It was your fault for being careless," retorted the captain pompously. "Money talks here in Firehara. The sultan despises poor people."

"This is outrageous!" Protested Aurnia angrily. "What are we supposed to do?"

"You're supposed to pay a fine, that's what you're supposed to do," replied Anders. "The penalty for vagrancy here in Firehara is a fine of two hundred gold pieces."

"But how can we possibly pay that?" Demanded Fang. "We don't have a penny."

"Well in that case you will just have to work off your debt in the salt mines!" Smiled the captain.

"The salt mines?" Replied Fenner in anguish. "How long will we have to work there for?"

"Like I said, until you have worked off your debt," snapped the captain.

"So how much do we get paid?" Asked Hector.

"You don't," said the captain flatly. "You will be slaves."

"But that means we'll be there forever!" Cried Lunar.

"Yes, I suppose it does," chuckled Anders.

"Well that's just really mean!" Cried Aurnia. "Everything about this city is vile and the people are the worst I have ever met!"

"Enough!" Barked the captain. He turned to the guards. "Take them to the cells," he instructed. "I believe one of their friends is already there. Put them in with him."

The friends were pushed and prodded towards the prison as Shuffler followed behind and laughed at them. Aurnia gripped her staff tightly. She was tempted to cast a bolt of lightning and send the guards scattering but that would only give them a little time to flee and there were still the high walls of the city to consider. Best to keep hold of the staff and wait for the right opportunity to use it, she thought to herself.

"That stick looks as though it could be used as a weapon," said one of the guards as he walked alongside her. "I had better take charge of it."

"But I've sprained my ankle and cannot walk without it," replied Aurnia quickly. The guard looked at her closely. Aurnia blushed; she was not good at lying but thankfully the guard seemed to believe her and didn't push the matter further. She made sure to put on a performance and hobbled the rest of the way.

Aurnia and her friends were led inside the prison and taken to One Flower's cramped corner cell. The camelolean smiled as the guard unlocked the door and ushered them inside. "Hey there princess friend is it visiting time again?" He said cheerfully.

"Not exactly," sighed Aurnia.

One Flower's face dropped. "Oh no!" He exclaimed. "You don't mean…"

"I'm afraid so," replied the princess as she sat down heavily on the wooden bench. "Just when we thought our luck couldn't get any worse."

Chapter Thirteen: The Torn Out Page

"I blame myself, friends," said One Flower sadly. "I should never have brought you here."

"On the contrary," replied Lunar. "It is us who should be saying sorry to you. If we hadn't come along you'd still be living quietly in your cottage by the river."

"Let's not get weighed down on blame," said Fang as he looked around the cell. "We need to find a way out of here."

"Oh there's no way out, my wolf friend," sighed One Flower. "We're going to the salt mines and that's that."

"Might we be able to escape from the salt mines?" Asked Hector.

"Oh no, never in a million years!" Replied the camelolean. "The salt mines are the worst place in the entire world. They make you get into this big rickety old elevator and take you hundreds of metres under the ground. Once you're there you never get out again – you even have to sleep down there. Nobody ever sees the light of day and nobody ever gets out!"

"We have to find a way!" Exclaimed Lunar. "I'm certainly not going to spend the rest of my life away from the forests of my homeland, out of sight of the moon forever."

Time passed by very slowly in the dark cell. After a while a sentry came along and dished out a thin gruel into wooden bowls. "You call this food?" Complained Fenner. "I could get a better meal out of the left over washing up water!"

"You might as well enjoy it whilst it lasts," taunted the sentry. "I hear the food is even worse in the mines."

"What a cheery thought," muttered the porcupine sarcastically.

After dinner the friends sat around glumly. There was nothing to do and they were very bored. "If only I could use my staff," sighed Aurnia. "But the only spell I really know is a lightning bolt and it is so powerful it might demolish the entire jail in the process."

"You know some other spells though," pointed out Fenner.

"I've used them but I don't know them," sighed Aurnia. "You know it is funny, I don't really know how I manage to conjure them up with my magical staff. It is like a power comes to me from within which I don't really know how to control. Perhaps it has something to do with my power as the Wolf of the Red Moon – but I can't seem to use that when I want to either."

The friends settled down as best they could but Aurnia remained restless. She climbed on to the bench and looked out of the barred window. In the distance, beyond the gateway, she could see the people of Firehara going about their business. She started to sing a mournful song.

"I can see a forest scene

Coming to me in my dreams

I close my eyes; I could be there

My home in Cominaer."

The verse continued:

"Yet time and time alone will tell

If we escape this dungeon cell

Oh! For the cold pine scented air

Of noble Cominaer."

Lunar now took up the song:

Oh moon above, now I'm not free

Will you shine brightly without me?

Bound for the mines and I despair

Of going back to Cominaer."

Now Fenner chipped in with a verse of his own:

"The gruel we get is thin and crude!

It really is disgusting food!

I wish I had a nice éclair!

Back home in Cominaer!

With the exception of Fenner's verse, which was rather silly and out of place, Aurnia thought they had made up a very tuneful, if rather depressing, song. The wolves howled mournfully as Aurnia sang the final verse:

"I dream the dreams of yesterday

And of my family far away

Oh spirits won't you heed my prayer?

And take me back to Cominaer."

"Hey! Stop that racket in there!" Came the angry voice of a guard from outside the cell. "If I hear any more of that din I shall come in there and throw a bucket of water over you!"

Aurnia sighed and went back to looking out of the window. The hours passed by and it got dark. They had spent almost the entire day inside this cell and a long night stretched ahead of them. Aurnia watched as the market traders and citizens went home for the day and the streets became quiet.

Aurnia rested her head on the window ledge and dozed off, only to awaken when something green jumped up on to the bars and started to slap her cheek with its front flippers. Aurnia opened her eyes quickly. "Guselin!" She exclaimed in astonishment. "What are you doing here?"

"What am I doing here? I have come to taunt you of course!" Replied the frog maliciously. "Imprisoned again I see; what an idiot! Aha! This is becoming quite a habit for you, isn't it? Well this time you will never escape!"

"Guselin?" Said Lunar as she came to the window. "My goodness, am I glad to see you!"

"How did you escape the sultan's palace?" Asked Aurnia eagerly.

"No walls can hold the mighty Guselin for long," replied the frog smugly.

Aurnia noticed Guselin was wearing a strange miniature backpack on his shoulders. It looked quite ridiculous and she wondered how he had come to acquire it. "So aren't the sultan's guards looking for you?" She asked him.

"Indeed they are!" Replied Guselin. "As we speak the hue and cry is being raised and the soldiers are scouring the streets in search of me. It is the most epic manhunt – or should I say frog-hunt – in the history of the world!"

Aunria peered out into the streets and listened. The city was eerily quiet. "I doubt whether they've even noticed he's missing," whispered Lunar. "And even if they have, he probably annoyed them so much they don't care."

"And how is Goldenmane?" Asked Aurnia.

"Pah! The foolish unicorn allowed himself to become enslaved!" Declared Guselin airily. "What do I care for him? He's an idiot!"

"But you were enslaved too," said Lunar reasonably.

"That is not so," snapped Guselin. "I am a master of my own fate! And besides, even if I was enslaved I escaped! And now I am here to taunt you! Yah-boo!" And with that he began to dance on his back legs whilst waving his front flippers in the air. Aurnia sighed, picked him up and took him inside the cell before placing him on the small table. The others were now awake and crowded around him.

"How did you get here?" Asked Fang. "How did you know where to find us?"

"Aha! I shall not tell!" Retorted Guselin rudely as he began to dance again. "I am not here to help you, just mock you! Foolish jailbirds!"

"I bet they were glad to see the back of you," said Fenner. "It is annoying enough being in prison without the frog coming to join us. Aren't we being punished enough?"

"Pah! I honour you with my presence!" Snapped Guselin defiantly. "I am so important! Why, your unicorn friend, Baron Silversnout, was begging me to run an errand for him barely an hour before I left!"

"What was that?" said Aurnia.

"Ah yes, he pleaded with me to come and find you and indeed I did," replied Guselin. "But you see I have deceived him! He wanted me to help you and give you the message he put in my backpack but I shall not! Not ever! I have come to gloat at your misfortune. Oh yes!"

Aurnia and Lunar exchanged glances. The princess seized hold of Guselin, flipped open his backpack and took out a tightly folded piece of paper. "This is an outrage!" Cried Guselin indignantly. "You will regret this, idiot princess! I shall bring about your doom!"

Aurnia set Guselin down on the table as she began to unfold the paper but the furious frog leapt up and tried to snatch it back. Carelessly the princess picked him back up and tossed him into the sink, which was half filled with stagnant water. "Aha! Paradise!" Exclaimed Guselin as he immediately forgot his bad temper and began to swim around happily. "All part of my plan!"

Aurnia finished unwrapping the piece of paper and began to study it closely. "What is it?" Asked Fenner eagerly. "Has Goldenmane sent us a note?"

"Not exactly," replied Aurnia as she squinted at the writing. "It appears to be a page torn from a book – a very old book by the looks of things. The writing seems to be for a spell of some sort. A spell for staffs."

"Staffs?" Repeated Hector. "Like the one you have here?"

"Let's hope so," replied the princess. "Goldenmane must have discovered the spell and sent Guselin to deliver it."

"Pah! He tried!" Exclaimed Guselin contemptuously. "But the mighty Guselin has no masters, only subordinates!"

"What kind of spell is it?" Asked Lunar, ignoring the frog's ranting.

"Some sort of transparency spell as far as I can tell," replied the princess.

"A transparency spell?" Said Fenner. "So for turning invisible you mean?"

"Yes and walking through walls," replied Aurnia.

"Ooh, that will be handy," said Hector.

"But it looks as though only the holder of the staff can use the spell," sighed Aurnia. "It would mean I had to leave the rest of you behind."

"That doesn't matter," replied Fang decisively. "You will be of far more use to us outside the prison. You must take this opportunity and escape."

"You mean leave you behind in this cell?" Said Aurnia uncertainly.

"Don't think of it like that," said Lunar kindly. "With you out of jail you can focus on finding a way to rescue us."

Aurnia sighed. She really didn't want to have to leave her friends but realised she had no other choice. "But what should I do when I am free?" She asked.

"Go and find Goldenmane and help him escape from the palace," suggested Fang. "Then make your way to the mines and find us. There must be a way out."

Aurnia gripped the staff and looked at the walls. "I could blast right through with a lighting spell," she said.

"But as you said before it would mean bringing down half the prison and there are so many guards about town we couldn't possibly get far and we'd never be able to rescue Goldenmane," said Fang. "No, Aurnia, I'm sorry but it has to be the transparency spell."

Aurnia nodded. "But when to go?" She asked.

"No time like the present," replied Fang. "At least it is night and quiet on the streets. Hopefully the transparency spell will shield you, but be careful all the same. You don't know how long it might last."

Aurnia studied the spell closely. "Well I can just about read it," she said at last. "I suppose I shall just have to give it a go and hope for the best." She picked up Guselin and slipped him into her knapsack pocket. "Here, you can come along for the ride. Just make sure you go to sleep and don't annoy me with your silly boasting."

"Aha!" Exclaimed Guselin happily as he settled down in the knapsack to go to sleep. "All part of my plan!"

"I don't suppose there is room for me in that knapsack as well?" Asked Fenner.

Aurnia shook her head sadly. "I'm afraid not," she replied.

Chapter Fourteen: Reunion With Lord Goldenmane

Aurnia gripped the staff as her friends looked on anxiously. She memorised the words on the page and began to chant the spell:

"Oh magic see me all concealed

Cause me to be unperceived

Make my appearance immaterial

Don me in a cloak ethereal"

"I don't know what most of those words mean," whispered Hector. "It must be a very clever spell."

The top of Aurnia's staff began to glow a bright yellow. The light slowly descended down the staff and covered it. Now Aurnia began to be enveloped by the light. The light grew brighter and brighter and the friends were forced to turn away. Lunar did not like this at all, for she was naturally afraid of anything that wasn't familiar to her.

All of a sudden the light vanished and the cell was plunged into darkness once more. Lunar turned and looked. There was no sign of the princess or the staff. "Aurnia?" Said the young wolf nervously. "Where did you go?"

"I'm here," came Aurnia's voice from the spot in which she had just been standing. "So you can't see me at all then?"

"Wow!" Exclaimed One Flower in astonishment. "That's some pretty impressive stuff!"

"It really worked then," said Fang. "I had my doubts but here I am seeing it with my own eyes – or not as the case may be."

For Aurnia this really was the strangest feeling. She could see her friends as plain as day but when she tried to look down at her own hands and feet there was nothing. She clapped her hands together and was relieved to find they were still there, even if she couldn't see them. She walked forwards slowly, reached out and tried to touch the wall but her hand slipped right through it. "Wow!" She exclaimed. "Did you see that? Oh no, clearly not. Goodness, this is very strange. I hope it isn't forever."

Fang went and looked over the spell on the table. "It won't be," he said reassuringly. "According to the spell you have about an hour. That means you will have to get going if you're going to reach the palace and Lord Goldenmane."

Aurnia said a reluctant goodbye to her friends. She did not like leaving them in the dungeon cell and she liked even less that there was nothing she would be able to do about them being transported to the salt mines in the morning.

"Goodbye and good luck, Aurnia," said Lunar.

"Thanks," replied the princess. She tried to hug the young wolf but her hands passed straight through. "I'm sure I will never stop making such silly mistakes," she sighed. "I am never going to get used to this."

With the good wishes of her friends ringing in her invisible ears, Aurnia took a deep breath and stepped through the prison wall.

The princess emerged on the other side of the wall and stepped into the courtyard. Beyond her was the street. It was late at night and the city was quiet. A guard turned the corner and walked right in front of her. Aurnia gave a start and almost stumbled back through the wall before realising her mistake. There was no need to hide when she was invisible! Aurnia hesitated and walked right up to the guard. He paid her not the slightest bit of attention; after all, how could he?

"Are you okay, Guselin?" Asked Aurnia after she had left the courtyard and walked a little way into the street. She stopped and listened and could hear the frog snoring in her invisible knapsack. She thought it best he remained asleep for now.

Aurnia began to walk through the streets in the direction of the palace. At this time of night, the only people about were patrolling guards on the lookout for thieves and vagrants. Aurnia walked right past them but kept her footsteps light, for even though she was invisible she could still be heard.

As the princess was passing by a rather rundown slum area a huge black wolf jumped right out in front of her and began a frenzied barking. Aurnia gave a cry but before she could react the wolf pounced at her, sailing right through where she was standing and landing in a heap behind her. Aurnia spun around as the wolf leapt up and crouched, drooling and snarling, its large yellow eyes fixed in terror.

"Easy there," said Aurnia uncertainly, but if she had hoped to calm the beast it had the opposite effect. The wolf began to bark with renewed frenzy, the noise alerting the guards. "Look, a vagrant!" Cried one of the guards as he notched an arrow in his bow and took aim. He let the arrow go and it sailed through the air and right through Aurnia, missing the wolf by an inch. As the guards drew their swords and gave chase the wolf turned and fled into a side alley. The guards followed, shouting and jeering. Aurnia carried on towards the palace.

As the princess approached the palace she saw a group of sentries standing guard outside. Aurnia walked right past them and passed through the door to find herself in the central hall. The reception area was deserted except for a hunched up figure lying asleep on the settee just outside the sultan's chambers. As Aurnia approached she saw it was Shuffler. Aurnia wondered what he was doing there. She gritted her teeth and her fists clenched. She was very angry with the him; he had betrayed them and caused them to be imprisoned and because of him her friends would be on their way to the salt mines in the morning. She was tempted to go and give him a good scare, knowing he would not be able to see her, but in the end she thought better of it. Like all bad apples he is bound to receive his comeuppance in time, she thought to herself.

Aurnia passed through the door and into the sultan's quarters. The lights were dimmed but she saw the sultan straight away sleeping on a big pile of cushions close to his throne. Two slaves were standing over him with fans, yawning and trying their hardest to stay awake.

Aurnia hesitated. She had no idea where she was going to start looking for Goldenmane. At the far end of the chamber, close to where the sultan was sleeping, was a pair of double doors. Aurnia walked through the doors and found herself in a long corridor. The corridor was nowhere near as grand as the rest of the palace and when Aurnia put her head through some of the doors she could see why, for these were clearly the slave quarters. As Aurnia looked in she saw cramped rooms in which the slaves were sleeping on bunk beds in uncomfortable looking woollen blankets. As she walked further down the corridor she paused and listened. Somewhere ahead there was a horse – or horse like creature – snoring loudly.

Aurnia went down some steps and came to a stout wooden door at the end of the corridor. The snoring was louder now. Aurnia put her head through the door and looked in. There was Goldenmane in a medium sized room that had been converted to a stable. There was straw on the floor, a trough filled with water in the corner, a small table and nothing else. Aurnia guessed the grand and pompous unicorn would not enjoy being housed in such a miserable looking room.

Goldenmane himself was asleep on his feet in the middle of the room, his head bowed. To Aurnia's surprise she saw his coat had been dyed a garish shade of pink whilst there were plumes and feathers entwined in his mane, which had been platted. He looked rather comical and not at all noble.

Aurnia looked back through the door to make sure nobody was coming then tiptoed over to the unicorn. "Goldenmane!" She whispered. "Wake up!"

Lord Goldenmane snorted with a start and opened his eyes. "What!" He exclaimed worriedly. "Who said that?"

"Keep your voice down!" Hissed the princess. "It is me, Aurnia."

"Aurnia?" Said Goldenmane. "But where are you hiding?" His eyes widened in understanding. "Of course!" He declared with a smile. "The magical spell! I don't know what surprises me more; that it actually worked or that the common little toad I sent actually did as I asked!"

"It worked alright but it is very strange being invisible and not even able to see my hands," said Aurnia.

"Strange for me too," replied Goldenmane. "You're just a voice coming out of thin air."

"How did you know we were in the dungeon?" Asked Aurnia. "How did you know where to send Guselin?"

"I happened to overhear that revolting slave boasting about it in the foyer," replied the unicorn. "He was telling everybody who would listen how he had gotten the better of you and had come to the palace hoping for a reward. As far as I know he's still here – the sultan declined to see him and for once I don't blame him. I'd want as little to do with the oik as well."

"You mean Shuffler," said Aurnia. "He double crossed us after we paid for his freedom."

"Yes well let that be a lesson never to rely upon the lower orders for anything," replied Goldenmane pompously. "Although as it turned out it was a good thing because it allowed me to pinpoint your location and send you the spell."

"How did you find the spell?" Asked Aurnia.

"Well it will come as no surprise to anyone that as a unicorn I am considered vastly superior to all the other lowly creatures who are forced to serve and toil here at the palace," boasted Goldenmane. "Even the sultan is in awe of me and has allowed me a certain amount of freedom. I have not had the opportunity to escape of course but I have been allowed the run of the palace and happened to come across the library yesterday morning. Whilst I was browsing through the books I found a very ancient volume on staff spells. The librarian would have noticed if I had stolen the book but whilst he wasn't looking I was able to tear out and conceal a couple of choice pages I thought might be helpful."

"It certainly was," said Aurnia gratefully. "So if the sultan was so in awe of you why did he make you dye your coat pink and put those silly things in your mane?"

"Oh!" Cried Goldenmane dramatically. "Even though the sultan has treated me better than his other underlings it has still been a most awful and humiliating experience for me! Why I am little more than a performing pony! Last night the sultan held a party and expected me to entertain. I tried to impress them with a unicorn poetry recital but they just laughed at my rhyming couplets and then the sultan made me do a humiliating sort of trot dance and everyone laughed some more!"

"I would have liked to have seen that," said Aurnia with a smile. "I does sound as though it would have been very funny."

"Well it wasn't!" Snapped Goldenmane crossly. He looked utterly crestfallen. "The sultan is vulgar and boisterous and he has the cruellest sense of humour I have ever seen. He treats all the slaves very badly indeed but it is worse for me because the slaves are common and I am not."

"Don't worry," Aurnia assured him. "We will soon find a way out of here."

"Ah yes," replied Goldenmane, brightening up somewhat. "Well as a matter of fact I've already thought of that."

"You have a plan?" Asked Aurnia eagerly but at that moment she felt a tingling sensation come over her. A bright yellow light flashed before her eyes and then cleared. Aurnia looked down at her hands and saw them clearly. The spell had worn off.

"Ah, there you are," said Goldenmane, seeing her for the first time that evening.

"Well this is inconvenient," said Aurnia. "Now I can't leave."

"You mean you cannot go out the way you came in," said Goldenmane knowingly. "Fortunately I have planned for that. Look on that side table over there."

Aurnia went over to the table and saw a single piece of paper with ancient looking writing on it. "Another page of the book!" She exclaimed. "But what is the spell?"

"It is a distraction spell," replied the unicorn. He made his way over to the window. Aurnia joined him and together they looked out at the silent moonlit city. "I have it all planned out," said the unicorn smugly. "After casting the distraction spell I shall flee over the rooftops with you riding upon my back. from there we shall leap on to the battlements and over the wall into the desert."

"But all the guards would have to be away from the walls," said Aurnia doubtfully.

"Yes, we will need quite a big distraction to divert their attentions," agreed Goldenmane thoughtfully.

"But how will we create such a big distraction?" Asked Aurnia.

At that moment Guselin peered out of the knapsack and smiled. "Aha! Trapped again, huh?" He declared maliciously. "Your puny human magic has worn off – I made it do that! Oh yes, just as I planned! Don't even dream of escape, it is quite futile. Aha!"

"Aha indeed!" Exclaimed Aurnia delightedly. "I have just the thing."

Chapter Fifteen: Escape Into The Desert

Day was dawning and the early traders were up and on their way to their stalls and markets. The soldiers were patrolling the streets and walls, ever alert for vagrants, thieves and anyone else who had earned the displeasure of the sultan.

All of a sudden a very frightened looking man came hurtling down the street towards the soldiers. "Run!" He cried in a panic. "Run for your lives!"

The soldiers looked around as he rushed past them. "What was that about?" Asked one of them.

In the middle distance there came a booming voice from behind a tall building. "Aha!"

Thundered the voice. "Now you will all feel my wrath!"

To the surprise and horror of the soldiers the earth shook and Guselin leapt around from behind the building to face them. The frog was the size of a medium sized house as he glared down at them. "This is great!" Cried Guselin. "This is brilliant! All part of my plan! Aha!"

The soldiers staggered backwards before turning tail. "Run!" Cried the second soldier. "Run for your lives!"

As the giant Guselin hopped down the central avenue pandemonium erupted amongst the people. Carts and market stalls were overturned and those who were too slow were almost trampled in the stampede to get away. "Aha! I will destroy you!" Yelled Guselin, who despite his threats seemed content to just hop up and down aimlessly. "You have no hope! Bow down and face my wrath!"

Meanwhile, from the palace window Aurnia was watching anxiously. "Well it certainly seems to be causing a distraction," she said to Goldenmane. "I just hope Guselin doesn't end up hurting anyone."

"That idiot frog doesn't have the brains to do any lasting harm," said Goldenmane as he pushed open the window with his nose. "Our plan is working perfectly. See how the soldiers are running down from the walls to leave them unguarded. Now let's go!"

Aurnia leapt upon Goldenmane's back and held on tightly. The unicorn backed up a little way before charging forwards and leaping out of the palace window and down on to the flat roof of a nearby house. It was a long way down and Aurnia was jolted as they landed and almost lost her balance. Somehow, she managed to hold on as Goldenmane swiftly found his feet and began to gallop as fast as he could, leaping from roof to roof with the city walls in his sights.

The sultan came out on to his balcony to see what all the noise was about. He gaped in astonishment as he saw the giant frog rampaging up and down the main street before noticing Goldenmane and Aurnia leaping from rooftop to rooftop as they tried to make good their escape. He rushed back inside and summoned the remaining soldiers. "Half of you go and subdue that frog, the rest get after the unicorn!" He yelled furiously. "I will not have my prize slave escaping!"

Some of the guards rushed out on to the palace balconies, bows and arrows at the ready. Aurnia was forced to crouch down as a volley of arrows whizzed past her head. Goldenmane noticed them too and began to gallop even faster.

Meanwhile, down on the main street, Guselin continued to cause a major distraction. "Aha! Now this town is mine!" He declared, and yet despite his increased power and the fear he was undoubtably causing amongst the people of Firehara, he only really seemed interested in being annoying. As people rushed away from a side street he deliberately leapt into a large muddy puddle and splashed them with filthy water. "Aha! You are soaked to the skin!" Taunted Guselin. "Now you will have to change!" He looked up and saw some clean white clothes drying on a washing line and kicked up some mud to go over the wall and cover them. "Now you will have to do it all again!" He exclaimed to the exasperated looking lady who came rushing out of her house to see what was happening.

Guselin now headed into the market and pushed over a stall, sending the hot pies on sale crashing into the mud. "My pies!" Cried the outraged stallholder. "I got up really early to bake those!"

"Aha! Your day is ruined!" Retorted Guselin.

The frog now hopped over a wall into a large garden and peered into the upstairs window where a very surprised old man gaped back at him from his bedroom. "Good morning! You are very ugly!" Mocked Guselin before hopping over the wall into the next garden where he spied a chicken coop. He reached out his froggy flipper and undid the latch before shooing all the hens out.

"Hey!" Cried an outraged old woman as she came hobbling out of the door. "What do you think you're playing at? That's very annoying! Now I will have to get them back in."

"Aha! I hope they eat all the plants in your garden!" Taunted Guselin before hopping on.

Meanwhile, Aurnia was holding on very tightly as Goldenmane leapt from roof to roof, arrows flying overhead as the archers targeted him from the palace balconies. The walls loomed before them. "Hold on tight!" Urged Goldenmane as he began to increase his speed.

"I've been holding on tight all the time!" Cried Aurnia. The unicorn leapt from the last rooftop and sailed through the air. The princess looked down and saw the street far below. She looked at the walls and for a moment thought they were not going to make it but at the last moment Goldenmane's front feet connected with the stonework and he kicked and scrambled his way up as Aurnia clung on for dear life.

Although most of the soldiers were down in the streets chasing after Guselin, there were still a few stragglers manning the battlements. Goldenmane charged through, knocking them aside as he went. Aurnia looked up and saw a group of soldiers forming up ahead, some with spears and swords at the ready, others aiming bows and arrows at point blank range. "Look out!" she cried.

"Time to get out of this accursed city once and for all!" Exclaimed Goldenmane as a torrent of arrows were loosed at them. The unicorn ducked sideways just in time and leapt from the castle walls. It was a very long way down. The desert floor rushed towards them. Aurnia held on tightly as they landed with a crash, the unicorn almost losing his footing before scrabbling to right himself and staggering forwards. Aurnia bounced up and down on his back, almost losing her grip and falling but the unicorn was able to right himself just in time and rushed off around the walls as another hail of spears and arrows rained down around them.

"How are we doing for time?" Panted Goldenmane as he galloped alongside the city walls.

"I'd say just about perfectly," replied Aurnia. "Or let's hope we did anyway. Here he comes right on schedule!"

Aurnia looked up as a huge shadow loomed over her. As if in slow motion Guselin leaped over the city walls and hurtled towards them. "Aha!" Cried the frog triumphantly. "All part of my plan!"

Guselin arced towards them and for a moment Aurnia was sure he was going to crush them but at the last second there came a flash of light. The magic of the distraction spell wore off in an instant. Guselin was back to his normal small self and landed neatly on the princess's shoulder. "Here he is!" Cried Aurnia. "Let's go!"

Goldenmane needed no more encouragement. He turned quickly and charged off into the desert, leaving the city walls behind and he didn't stop running until they were well out of sight over the horizon.

Chapter Sixteen: A Pact With The Jackals

"Its okay, Goldenmane," said Aurnia as she looked behind them. "Nobody is following us. You can slow down now."

The unicorn was sweating and panting as he slowed to a trot. "Can't... go... another step!" He wheezed.

"Just a few more," urged Aurnia. "Look over there." She pointed towards a small oasis amongst the dunes. Goldenmane smiled weakly. "The spirits smile upon us," he muttered.

Goldenmane staggered to the oasis and waded straight into the water to cool down. Aurnia slipped off his back and took a long drink. Guselin leapt off her shoulder and began to swim around gleefully, rising for a moment to spit water at Goldenmane before diving right back down again.

"Disgusting common frog!" Snapped the unicorn crossly. "You're swimming in my drinking water!"

"Stupid uppity horse!" Snapped Guselin defiantly as he rose to the surface. "The mighty Guselin saved the day!"

"Indeed you did," agreed Aurnia. "And we are very grateful to you but all the same think of everything you could have done with that power. You might have gone to the palace and taken on the sultan himself but from what I saw of you when we were galloping over the rooftops you were just annoying as usual."

"You are a fool to underestimate the mighty Guselin!" Snapped the frog crossly. "Everything he does it all part of his grand plan! Oh yes!"

"You are an idiot," snapped Goldenmane dismissively. "Just as well you are sometimes a useful idiot or I would favour leaving you in the nearest mud puddle we come across. In fact, you would probably be very happy there because you are nothing more than a common little toad."

After he had swum around and annoyed them both some more, Guselin climbed into the knapsack pocket and settled down to sleep. Aurnia and Goldenmane settled down to rest beneath the shade of a tree. The princess thought about her friends and how they would now be on their way to the mines. She wondered how they were going to rescue them but she was too tired to work out a plan right now. She closed her eyes and had soon fallen into a deep sleep.

Aurnia was the first to wake. To her surprise she realised she had been sleeping for most of the day, for the sun was going down quickly and the temperature was falling. She got up and stretched. Goldenmane also stirred and woke. He went down to the oasis and began to drink. Aurnia joined him.

"We seem to have overslept," said Aurnia.

"That doesn't matter," replied Goldenmane dismissively. "It will be far more comfortable to travel by night and we are less likely to be discovered by the hunting parties the sultan is bound to have sent out. Where are the mines anyway? How far do we have to go?"

Aurnia frowned. "Actually I have no idea," she replied.

"What do you mean you have no idea?" Demanded the unicorn irritably.

"I thought you'd know," replied the princess. "After all, you've been to the library."

"Well I didn't exactly think to go rummaging amongst the maps!" Snapped Goldenmane. He sighed. "This is great. We are going to be wandering around this arid wasteland forever at this rate."

Aurnia heard something coming up very fast behind her. She went to turn around but it was too late. Something crashed into her hard and sent her rolling to the ground. She looked up to see a group of jackals converging upon Goldenmane who reared up on his hind legs and kicked out at them. Another jackal ran to her resting place and seized her staff in its mouth to prevent her from using it like before. Soon Goldenmane had been subdued and forced back against the bank of the oasis alongside Aurnia. The jackals encircled them. The pack leader, Whispera, stepped forwards to confront them. "Ah! So you were fool enough to return were you?" Growled the jackal threateningly. "Once more you trespass upon our land and steal our water and shade."

"We mean you no harm and we never did," protested Aurnia. "And it is like I said before, we would not survive out in this desert without this water and shade."

"Yes and we never chose to come to this accursed horrible place!" Added Goldenmane. "You are welcome to this dump for all I care!"

Whispera scowled at the unicorn and turned back to Aurnia. "Where are the rest of you?" She demanded.

"They were taken prisoner after we were doubled crossed in Firehara," replied the princess.

"And how did you two manage to escape?" Asked the pack leader.

"That's a long story," replied Aurnia.

"I bet it is," snapped Whispera. "And I'm betting it had something to do with this magical staff of yours." She looked towards the staff which was being closely guarded by three strong jackals. "Well if your friends have been taken prisoner there is little hope for them. The sultan is a very harsh fellow as we jackals know only too well."

"Yes, our friends are being sent to the mines as we speak," replied Aurnia.

"The salt mines, huh?" Muttered Whispera. She grimaced. "I wouldn't wish that on anyone no matter how much they have disrespected my people."

"Disrespected your people?" Put in Goldenmane rudely. "How did we disrespect you common jackals? By not dying of thirst in this awful desert?

You don't own the sand; you don't own anything. You're just a bunch of common vagrants — even more common than wolves in my opinion. At least wolves have the good sense to live in the forests where it is cool and shady."

"What did you call us?" Snarled Whispera as the angry jackals closed in around them.

"Enough!" Cried Aurnia in exasperation. "We have been through too much already in Firehara. Can't we all just get along? Perhaps you could even help us?"

"Help you?" Repeated Whispera. She laughed harshly. The rest of the pack joined in. "You have some cheek to ask us for help after what you did."

"What do you mean after what we did?" Snapped Goldenmane. "We didn't do anything."

"You blasted us with that staff," retorted Whispera.

"Oh yes, well I suppose there was that," acknowledged Goldenmane begrudgingly. "But that was only because you were chasing us."

"We might have been seriously hurt," retorted Whispera.

"Yes but unfortunately you weren't," muttered the unicorn.

"What did you say?" Demanded the jackal angrily.

"Just ignore my horse," said Aurnia quickly. "He can be very rude sometimes."

"I beg your pardon?" Said Goldenmane, sounding quite outraged.

"Enough!" Snapped Whispera sternly. "I have decided I don't care about your friends. You have wronged us and it is time to pay so we are going to take you hostage."

"And just what does that mean?" Demanded Goldenmane. He had already been imprisoned once on this adventure and he was in no hurry to experience it again so soon.

"You are both coming with us," said the pack leader. She nodded to the other jackals who now formed a tight ring around them.

"And where are we going?" Asked Aurnia.

Whispera considered for a moment and looked around. "Well actually we might as well stop here for a while," she said. "There isn't another oasis about for many miles."

"Where do you actually live?" Asked Aurnia. "Is it far from here?"

"Where do we live? We live here," replied Whispera, motioning with her nose. "This whole desert is our home. We wander where we choose and sleep where we want."

Goldenmane snorted contemptuously. "Even for wolf type creatures you are especially common and stupid," he scoffed. "Imagine calling this vile sandpit your home and not even having the wit to make yourselves a hole in the ground."

"You are being very annoying!" Growled Whispera threateningly.

"Enough! Both of you!" Snapped Aurnia crossly. She went and sat back down against the tree, the jackals watching her closely. On the other side of the oasis she saw two of the creatures curiously examining her staff. She hoped they didn't cast a spell by mistake and do some damage.

The princess wrapped her arms around herself and shivered. It was very cold and she doubted she would get back to sleep again. She thought about her friends in the mines and all the time being wasted whilst the jackals waylaid them. If only she could think of a way to get her magical staff back.

The wind whipped up and swirled the sand around them. Aurnia blinked and cried out. "Ow!" she cried as she staggered to her feet. "I've got sand in my eyes!"

Whispera looked at her unsympathetically. "What a foolish girl," she snapped. "It serves you right."

"I can't see!" Exclaimed the princess. She put her hands out in front of her and staggered from side to side. "Ow! Ow! This really stings!"

A jackal named Luxin got up and approached her. "Here, hold on to me," he said. "I will take you to the oasis and you can wash it out."

"Thanks," said Aurnia appreciatively. She held on to Luxin as he led her into the water and immediately waded straight in. "Hey!" Cried the jackal in surprise. "Surely you're not going for a swim at this time of night?"

The princess paid no attention. Instead she dived down under the water and was immediately lost to sight. Whispera got up from under a tree and came over to the oasis. "Hey, where did she go?" Demanded the pack leader.

Goldenmane also came down to the water's edge. The pool was dark and still. They waited and waited but she did not emerge. "Aurnia?" Said Goldenmane worriedly.

Whispera and Luxin waded a little way into the water and looked around. "What is she playing at?" Wondered Luxin.

All of a sudden there came a loud splash from the other side of the bank as Aurnia burst out of the water, rolled on to the bank and made a grab for her staff. The jackals were too slow to react and Aurnia seized it up just in time and immediately bounced a bolt of lightning off the ground that had them staggering back.

"Back!" Cried Aurnia as she waved the staff threateningly over her head. "Back I say!"

Goldenmane waded into the oasis and came to join her on the other side of the bank. "Well this evens the score," he said smugly.

"I can see we have underestimated you," snarled Whispera. "How does one as young as you wield such awesome power?"

"I don't quite understand it myself," replied the princess.

"Come on, Aurnia," said Goldenmane. "Let's get out of here and leave this common rabble behind."

"Yes, get out of here," growled Whispera. "You have caused us nothing but trouble and we will be glad to see the back of you."

Aurnia went to climb on Goldenmane's back before hesitating and turning back to the pack leader. "We don't know the way to the mines," she said. "Perhaps you would reconsider and help us after all?"

"Why would we help you?" Scoffed Luxin. "Let's face it, we are not exactly friends."

"Friends, no, but we have a common enemy in the sultan of Firehara," replied the princess reasonably.

"Whispera frowned. "You know nothing of our fight," she muttered.

"We know the sultan is a tyrant who keeps many of his people enslaved," said Aurnia. "We know too he is a deceiver and an all-round bully."

"Yes, and he imprisoned our friends and is sending them to the salt mines," added Goldenmane.

"Why do you jackals dislike the sultan so much?" Asked Aurnia.

Whispera frowned. "We jackals used to be welcome in Firehara," she said. "We kept the streets free of rats and in return the market traders would feed us scraps and allow us to sleep under their stalls at night. That was until the current sultan came to the throne and declared that we were vagabonds. He said he would make his slaves deal with the rats and threw us out of the city, forcing us to become nomadic. We have had to learn quickly how to hunt and scavenge in the desert."

"Then help us," urged Aurnia. "We do not just want to free our friends, we want to free all the slaves as well and we can only do that by overthrowing the sultan himself."

"Overthrow the sultan you say?" Muttered Whispera thoughtfully. She glanced over to Luxin who nodded. "It is a grave fate to be made to work the mines," said the pack leader after a while. "As it happens my brother, Pauna, is also there."

"Your brother?" Said Aurnia.

"That's right," replied Whispera. "He was captured last year trying to sneak into the city to attend a secret rebel meeting held in a camelolean's café. As soon as I heard he had been taken to the mines I gave up hope."

"But why?" Asked Goldenmane. "Surely there was something you could have done?"

"There are over two thousand slaves working those mines and they are very heavily guarded," said Luxin. "Breaking anybody out would be an impossible undertaking."

"Perhaps under normal circumstances but I am wondering about this staff," said Whispera thoughtfully. "If the girl can find a way to control it perhaps it contains the power we need to give us victory."

"And that is not all," said Goldenmane proudly. "Princess Aurnia is also the Wolf of the Red Moon."

Whispera and Luxin looked at one another. "The Wolf of the Red Moon is a legend," said Luxin doubtfully. "It does not exist."

"What common out of touch creatures you are," snapped Goldenmane haughtily. "Do you know nothing about what has been happening in the world of late?"

"You keep getting on my nerves, pack-pony," snarled Whispera.

"Hey!" Cried Goldenmane indignantly.

"Well regardless of whether you are the Wolf of the Red Moon we have seen the power of this staff for ourselves," said Luxin.

"Yes, and I might not get a chance to see my brother again," said Whispera thoughtfully. "I am not keen to trust you but I cannot pass up this opportunity or I might regret it for the rest of my life." She sighed and turned to the pack. "We are going to the mines," she announced. The other jackals barked their approval.

Aurnia and Goldenmane packed up their oasis camp and made ready to leave with Whispera and her pack. "I don't like this one bit," muttered Goldenmane. "These jackals have hardly treated us fairly and to make matters worse they outnumber us at least ten to one! What if they try to make a grab for the staff when you're not ready? I'm starting to think we might have been better off leaving them behind. Remember too we haven't been able to trust a single creature since we weighed anchor in this accursed desert world."

"What about One Flower?" Replied Aurnia. "We can trust him."

"Pah! We couldn't trust the fool not to get arrested straight away!" Retorted the unicorn. "It was because we tried to help him that we ended up in this predicament in the first place."

"I don't think the jackals will harm us," said the princess. "They might not like us very much but they like the sultan even less. They're sensible enough to realise they won't get very far without the help of the staff and I'm the only one who knows how to use it."

"I just hope you're right," sighed Goldenmane.

Chapter Seventeen: Into The Mines

Aurnia climbed on to Goldenmane's back and they set off. Aurnia looked around uneasily. There were over twenty jackals accompanying them and she did not trust them at all. It still felt as though they were under guard. She gripped the staff tightly and hoped she would not need to use it on them, for she was sure they were good creatures at heart who had been badly wronged by the wicked sultan.

The party moved through the desert at a brisk pace. "How far do we have to go?" Asked Goldenmane.

"The mines are several miles to the west of Firehara," replied Whispera. "We will be travelling most of the night but I hope to be there before sunrise."

On through the desert they went. As they travelled the jackals sang a mournful song.

"Banished by the sultan's law.

Forced to live on the desert floor

Now we travel by the moon

Casting shadows from the dunes

Desert homeland!

Proud our pack stands!

Onwards lupines of the sand!

Marching forwards as one pack

Off to get our brother back

We were crushed but now revolt

In the mines of tin and salt

See the flames fanned!

Make a last stand!

Onwards lupines of the sand!"

"What a common song," said Goldenmane critically after they had finished.

"Oh I don't know, I thought it was rather epic," said Aurnia.

As they continued on through the desert Aurnia looked down at her staff. "I would be interested in studying that book of spells myself," she said.

"As you should be," replied Goldenmane. "It was a most fascinating volume bound in ancient leather and there were all kinds of spells contained within. I found out something about your staff too. It seems as though it is very ancient and was carved from the wood of an enchanted tree which grew in the glade of the spirits. From what I can gather it was the first tree that ever existed – the tree from which all the other plants of the world took seed. Amazing how much there is to learn about this world of ours don't you think?"

"I certainly do," agreed Aurnia.

A short while later Guselin poked his head out of the knapsack pocket. "Aha! So the jackals I sent succeeded in capturing you huh?" He taunted.

"Oh, there you are," said Aurnia flatly. "I forgot all about you and might have left by the oasis."

"Yes and as it happens the jackals are our friends now," added Goldenmane. "So there; shows what you know."

"Aha! They are planning to deceive you like I instructed!" Laughed Guselin. "I can't believe you have been taken in so easily."

"Be quiet," snapped Aurnia. "You're such a pest do you know that? If you don't keep your voice down the jackals might not realise you're just an idiot and take you seriously."

"As well they should! Oh yes!" Cried the frog. "Anyway, where are we going?"

"To the mines to rescue the others," replied Aurnia.

"You will never succeed!" Declared Guselin gleefully. "You are doomed and so are they! All of your friends! You will never see Finbert, Looter, Tooth or Harvey the talking cow ever again, do you hear me? You yourselves will be enslaved and will remain there forever. It is all part of my plan; oh yes! Aha!"

"Do you ever give it a rest?" Snapped Goldenmane crossly. "And can it really be the case that you've been adventuring with us for so long and don't yet know our names?"

"Be quiet, Duke Silverfoot, I know all there is to know!" Snapped Guselin.

"Talking of giving it a rest you seem to spend most of your life resting," said Aurnia. "I have never known a creature to sleep as much as you. Not that I'm complaining of course. When you are awake all you ever do is annoy."

"Yes, sleeping is the only time I can tolerate you," sniped Goldenmane.

"Do not belittle me, idiots!" Retorted Guselin angrily. "I will bring about your doom!"

"And so it goes on," sighed Aurnia.

After travelling for a long time the princess saw the towers of Firehara in the distance. The jackals changed course and kept well clear of the city so they were not discovered by any of the sultan's patrols. They walked for a long time but after a while the ground became firmer. Hills of hard sand distinct from the dunes rose up before them. "How much longer?" Groaned Goldenmane.

Whispera looked up at the moon. "Not much further now," she replied as she motioned towards a tall hill. "Just over that ridge and we should see the entrance."

The party climbed the hill to the top of the ridge. Aurnia looked down. Before her was the mining complex, dug out of a tall hill. There were tracks, shafts and wooden buildings dotted all around and as she looked she saw groups of soldiers patrolling back and forth. "So there it is," she murmured.

"Indeed," replied Whispera gravely. "The final home many poor creatures will ever know." She shuddered.

"It doesn't seem big enough," said the princess.

"Looks can be deceptive," said Luxin. "Underground is a vast network of tunnels and caverns reaching down three levels."

"It is certainly well guarded," said Goldenmane worriedly. "How are we going to get in?"

"We will need to create a distraction," said Whispera thoughtfully.

"You mean like another distraction spell?" Asked Aurnia.

"No spells," replied the pack leader firmly. "Anything too unusual and they will send to Firehara for reinforcements."

"Then what?" Demanded Goldenmane.

Whispera thought for a moment then turned around to her pack. "We cannot all infiltrate the mines," she declared to them. "We cannot possibly overwhelm all these soldiers even with the magical staff. Therefore, myself and Luxin will join the girl and the horse and find a way to sneak inside whilst the rest of you make a raid on the canteen shed to the left of the entrance."

"I'm sorry!" Exclaimed Goldenmane indignantly. "What did you just call me?"

"Be quiet!" Hissed Aurnia. "Let Whispera speak. Her plan depends on everyone working together."

"Make it look like an ordinary food raid," continued Whispera to her pack. "Go in, snatch what you can and let the soldiers chase you off. Try to draw it out for a couple of minutes to give the four of us plenty of time."

The jackals readily agreed to the plan and began to sneak down towards the canteen shed, ready to attack. "Now then," said Whispera. "When I give the signal we shall head for the central shaft."

"And then what?" Asked Goldenmane.

"I'm not sure exactly," replied Whispera warily. "That's why the princess had better keep the staff close to hand. You never know when you might need to use it."

Aurnia, Goldenmane, Whispera and Luxin watched as the jackals came down from the ridge in a long snaking line. "This is a common thing for hungry jackals to do," explained Whispera. "It will cause a scene but not too much alarm."

Aurnia watched as the jackals aligned themselves into an arrow formation and started to run. The soldiers patrolling the perimeter saw them and cried out but were quickly knocked aside as the jackals headed straight for the canteen sheds. "Get ready," muttered Whispera.

As the jackals rushed into the sheds more soldiers rushed to confront them. "Now!" Said Whispera.

Aurnia, Goldenmane and the two jackals hurried down from the ridge. Aurnia looked around her, staff held tightly. Meanwhile from inside the sheds there came the sounds of shouts and howls as soldier and jackal confronted one another.

The dark central shaft loomed before Aurnia. What would they find inside, she wondered. For thousands of slaves this was the last time they were out in the open air; their last ever sight of the sky. The princess gritted her teeth and ran, her face fixed in determination as she hurried into the dark entranceway. She did not know what they would find down in the mines but she was determined to rescue not only her friends but also every single slave who was forced to toil here. The sultan was going to pay for his cruelty. Of that there could be no doubt.

Chapter Eighteen: A Dangerous Reunion

A long rectangular tunnel stretched off into the distance. The walls of the mine were smooth and white and gave off a strange natural light which meant there was no need for candles.

"Quickly!" Exclaimed Whispera. "Before the guards come back."

The two jackals led the way along the tunnel which began to wind downwards beneath the mountain. Ahead of them they heard footsteps. Whispera ushered them into an alcove and they crouched down and waited as a party of three guards rushed past to join the battle outside. Once they were out of sight they continued along the main passageway. Every now and again Whispera would stop to sniff the air before urging them onwards.

"I haven't seen any slaves yet," said Goldenmane.

"It is still night and they will probably be resting," replied Whispera. "Only a few select slaves are allowed to work the carts along the tracks. The others are kept on the lower levels. Come on, we need to find an elevator of some sort."

After continuing along the main passageway for some time the pack leader led them down a side corridor and into a small room containing hats and coats. "This must be some sort of resting room for the overseers," said Whispera. "This is just what we need. Come on, let's disguise ourselves."

"You want me to dress up as an overseer?" Scoffed Goldenmane. "Preposterous! Nobody will ever believe it! I am far too noble and dignified!"

"You are quite right," agreed Luxin. "Nobody will ever believe you are an overseer but if you cover up your horn with one of these helmets you might just pass for a packhorse."

"A packhorse!" Cried Goldenmane in outrage. "How dare you!"

"It will only be for a short while," Aurnia reassured him as she put on a hat and coat which was far too big for her. "Although even in disguise I'm afraid we will draw suspicion."

"That's why we still need to keep out of sight wherever possible," said Whispera. "Keep your heads down and don't talk to anyone unless you absolutely have to."

Aurnia helped the jackals to put on wraparound leather helmets which allowed their ears to stick out, then found the largest hat she could and put it over Goldenmane's head to cover his horn. It looked rather comical but would have to do for now, she thought. "What indignity!" Groaned the unicorn wretchedly. "The things I have to do to be a hero!"

Once everyone was dressed the party left the rest room and headed back out into the central corridor.

"How will we know where our friends are?" Asked Aurnia.

"All newcomers are taken straight to the third level — that is to say the bottom level," replied Luxin. "This is the hardest level of all. The slaves are worked eighteen hours per day and are only allowed one meal. The idea is that they work hard to be promoted to the second and first levels, which are supposed to be easier."

"What happens if you work hard on the first level?" Asked Goldenmane.

"Nothing," replied Whispera darkly. "The slaves are here for life."

"If they are right at the bottom level it will be even harder to get them out," sighed Goldenmane.

"This is true," replied Whispera. "But don't despair. There should be a central elevator shaft around here somewhere which will take us straight there."

The four of them walked single file, keeping their heads as low as possible. They heard voices coming up fast behind them. Aurnia held her breath. "Guards!" Hissed Whispera as she looked behind her. "Just ignore them and don't make eye contact."

"Those jackals are so annoying," said one of the soldiers crossly as he walked past them. "They got three sacks of food this time - if you ask me the sultan ought to order them chased out of the desert altogether."

"At least we were able to deal with them," replied the second soldier. "I would have liked to have caught one of the pests but it is as well they ran away. Hopefully after the hiding we just gave them they will think twice about trying to rob us again."

At that moment the first soldier turned his head and looked straight at Aurnia. The princess froze and looked back at him, hoping the fear didn't show in her eyes. The soldier narrowed his eyes suspiciously. Aurnia gripped her staff, ready to cast a spell but at the last moment the fellow moved his gaze away and carried on down the passageway with his friend. Before long they had rounded the corner and were lost to sight. Aurnia and her friends breathed a sigh of relief.

The party continued deep into the mines. Aurnia realised they must be deep under the mountain by now. From around the corner a cart full of salt appeared. The cart was being pushed by four cameolean slaves. An overseer was following behind. As they approached the overseer looked them up and down. His expression hardened in suspicion and he opened his mouth to say something but at that moment Luxin leapt forwards and snapped at the ankles of one of the slaves who cried out in shock. "Faster there!" Barked the jackal harshly. "The markets of Firehara are waiting for that salt!"

The slaves began to run with the cart, whimpering with fear. The overseer nodded at Luxin as he walked past. "I didn't like to do that but I am afraid it was necessary," said Luxin sadly. "The overseer was about to challenge us. Once we have freed the slaves of this mine I shall seek out the fellow I wronged and make amends."

A short while later Aurnia, Goldenmane and the two jackals came to an elevator at a crossroads. It was a very large and rickety looking wooden contraption with spokes and pulleys to control it and it didn't look very safe at all. To the side of the elevator was a very large wheel with bars on either side. Inside was a very thin and tired looking jackal who was running on the wheel to lower it.

"Pauna!" Exclaimed Whispera in astonishment. She rushed over to the wheel. Pauna looked at her in astonishment. "Whispera!" He exclaimed. "And Luxin too! What happened? Have you been captured?"

"Not by a long shot," replied the pack leader happily. "We are here to save you."

"Good luck," sighed Pauna. "I am locked in this cage and only a fat cameolean on the lower levels has the key."

"You are so much thinner than you were before," said Luxin sadly. "The sultan's overseers must be working you very hard."

"I barely get a moment of rest all day," sighed Pauna. "It has been the same from the moment I arrived here. I don't know how much more of this I can take."

"This ends today," said Whispera determinedly. "We are going to find a way to get you out."

Aurnia went over to the wheel and examined the lock. She smiled and gripped her staff. "No problem," she said. "Stand back everyone."

Aurnia readied her staff and concentrated. A red hot glow came from the top of the staff, the heat almost too much for the princess to bear. She touched the staff to the lock and it immediately snapped and broke, falling to the floor with a clatter.

"Astonishing," breathed Pauna as he gratefully stepped out of the wheel. "I had always thought escape from this place was quite impossible.

"Not with the princess and her magical staff," said Whispera proudly. She briefly explained their plan to free all the slaves from the mine and overthrow the sultan.

"Ah yes, I think I remember your friends," said Pauna thoughtfully. "They came here yesterday and were taken straight to the lower level."

"Can you take us to them?" Asked Aurnia hopefully.

"I can certainly take you to the lower level," said the jackal. "But I do not know exactly where they are. Almost certainly working in one of the side tunnels I should say." He thought for a moment. "I had better stay with the wheel," he said. "I should be able to delay the guards for a while by not bringing the elevator up to them although there are other ways down so be careful."

Aurnia, Goldenmane and the two jackals entered the elevator. Pauna began to turn the wheel slowly, his expression pained. The princess could only imagine what he had been through these past few months. Slowly the elevator began to descend.

"I don't like being this far underground," muttered Whispera worriedly.

Aurnia could well understand this fear, for the jackal was a lupine creature and she was sure Lunar felt exactly the same worry at being out of sight of the moon for so long.

The elevator shook and shuddered before coming to an abrupt stop that had Aurnia and her friends staggering back and forth. Pauna closed his eyes and panted. "This is the last level," he grunted.

"What an awful life they have made you live," said Whispera sympathetically. "I don't know how you have managed it for so long."

"I just want to see the sun and the moon again," sighed Pauna sadly.

"And you will, very soon," Aurnia assured him. "We are going to rescue my friends and overthrow the wicked sultan once and for all."

"I hope so," said Pauna. "I will wait here for you to return and make sure nobody tries to take the elevator up. If there is trouble I will howl an alarm."

"And we will come running," Luxin assured him.

"Just be careful," said Pauna. "This level of the mine is extremely well guarded. Escape will be very difficult, let alone rebellion. May the full moon guide you."

Aurnia, Goldenmane and the jackals said goodbye to Pauna and stepped out into the mines. They walked along a long passageway flanked by tunnels in the walls leading upwards. From the tunnels came the sound of pickaxes chipping away at the rock and every now and again hard lumps of salt would fall down. Slaves trundled carts back and forth, scooping up the salt in shovels and taking it off to a storage area ready to be transported to the surface.

"What a dismal life this must be," remarked Goldenmane with a shudder. He watched as a slave scurried back and forth, shovelling the salt into his cart before rushing off with it along the tracks. "Look how hard he is working."

"The slaves are told they have to collect a certain amount of salt every day," explained Luxin. "If they don't meet their quota they don't get fed."

"How awful," said Aurnia sadly. "The more I hear about this sultan's tyrant rule the more I dislike him."

As they continued along the passageway they saw many more tunnels cut into the rock. "To think there are slaves in each one of them," said Luxin sadly.

"Why there are hundreds of them," sighed Goldenmane. "We will never find the others at this rate. We don't know where to begin to start looking."

Aurnia looked ahead and saw three guards marching along the passageway. The passageway was very narrow at this point which meant the guards came very close to Aurnia and her friends. The first guard paused and looked at them closely. "Wait a minute," he said suspiciously. "I haven't seen you four around here before."

"We just started today," replied Whispera in a loud and confident voice.

"Is that so?" Muttered the guard. "Well I am in charge at this level and am supposed to be kept informed of any new overseers around here." He peered at them closely. "It is certainly strange to see two jackals and a child made overseers of the third level. Strange too that these three overseers should be in the company of an ordinary packhorse."

"It must have been an oversight on your part," said Luxin tensely.

"Not likely," snorted the soldier. He turned to his comrades. "Guard them closely," he instructed. "I'm going up to the surface to check this out for myself."

"I think not!" Declared Goldenmane defiantly and with that he spun around and kicked out with his powerful back legs. His feet connected with the chest of the first soldier, sending him flying back into the other two. The three of them crashed against the wall opposite and slid to the floor in a daze.

"Wow!" Exclaimed Luxin. "That was quite something."

A slave rounded the corner with a wagon half filled with salt. He stopped short when he saw the three soldiers lying sprawled on the floor, his mouth dropping open in horror. Aurnia hurried over to him. "We have come from the surface to rescue you all," she said quickly. "Please do not give us away. Put these soldiers in your cart and carry them somewhere safe where they will not be found."

The slave considered for a moment before agreeing, dragging the soldiers up and into the wagon.

"Wait a moment," said Goldenmane as the slave turned to leave. The unicorn concentrated hard. His horn began to glow a shining yellow and enveloped the three unconscious guards for several seconds before fading. Goldenmane staggered back, a pained expression upon his face. He seemed a little weaker than before.

"What was that?" Asked Whispera.

"Lord Goldenmane just used his unicorn healing magic on them," explained Aurnia. "Now when they wake up they won't be injured."

"And there was I thinking you were just a horrible pompous old stick in the mud," said Whispera.

"Oh no, Goldenmane is very noble. He gave those soldiers his magic even though it hurts him to use it," replied Aurnia proudly.

"Humph! And don't you forget just how noble a creature I am!" Muttered Goldenmane. They waited a while to allow him to regain his strength before carrying on down the passageway.

"How are we going to find them?" Wondered Goldenmane. "We can't search all these passageways."

"No, and time is short," agreed Whispera. "Sooner or later those guards will be missed."

At that moment, from a tunnel just to the side of them, they heard a mournful out of tune singing.

"My pickaxe!

Hammering salt from the hard stone!

Our own homes!

Will we ever go back?"

That's Fenner's awful singing!" Exclaimed Aurnia excitedly. They listened as the song continued.

"Oh sadly!

The sultan says that we did wrong!

The days long!

When will we be free?"

"Here," said Aurnia. "It is coming from this tunnel."

"Well I will never fit up there," said Goldenmane as he looked at the narrow entranceway.

"You won't have to, I will go alone," said Aurnia. "You three go a little way from here and look busy so you don't attract the attention of anymore guards."

As Goldenmane and the two jackals went off Aurnia, entered the tunnel and began to climb upwards. Every now and again large rocks of salt would tumble down and she was forced to scramble out of the way. The princess climbed for a long time. The salt in the air made her mouth dry and she felt very thirsty.

Eventually the tunnel widened out into a small cavern. Ahead of her were One Flower, Hector, Fenner, Lunar and Fang. Hector and One Flower were chipping at the rock with their picks whilst Lunar and Fang were digging with their claws. Fenner was doing no work at all but instead was sat back against a rock singing about how bad things were here in the mines.

"We poor slaves!

Work all day as stone cutters!

Oh! What times supper?

When will we be saved?"

"Right now!" Exclaimed the princess dramatically.

The others spun around. "Aurnia!" Cried Lunar happily as she ran over to hug her.

Everyone was delighted to see Aurnia again and she in turn was very pleased to see them. Once they had greeted one another Aurnia told them all about her adventures since she had cast the transparency spell and walked through the walls of the jail.

"We got here yesterday afternoon and got put to work straight away," said Fenner. "It is awful. We are either working or sleeping and there is very little time given to eating! And even when we are fed the food is so bland it is hardly worth bothering with, which is ironic considering we're working in a salt mine."

"I don't like chipping rock at all, princess friend," sighed One Flower unhappily. "But then I don't think I'd like it even if we were being paid. Attacking things with a pickaxe is all just too violent for me, like we are somehow attacking the mountain. I've always been a creature of peace, you know?"

"Worst of all is Fenner's constant singing," added Lunar. "He's just so out of tune and annoying and he just won't stop! An overseer even came by and poked him with a stick but he still wouldn't stop!"

"What can I say? It takes a lot to break the porcupine spirit," said Fenner with a shrug.

"Well now I am here with the staff," said Aurnia. "We can stir up a revolt of the slaves and escape from this place."

"Not so fast!" Came a familiar voice from behind them.

Aurnia spun around. "Shuffler!" She exclaimed in horror. "What are you doing here?"

"That's Slave Master Shuffler to you, girl!" Retorted Shuffler arrogantly.

"A slave master?" Said Aurnia. "You mean you are now working for the sultan as his overseer? I cannot believe it after all you suffered as a slave."

"Oh he's the worst," sighed One Flower with a shudder. "He came to the mines with us and he's taken an especial disliking to us friends!"

"Yes, he's made our lives an absolute misery," added Fang. "He makes us do twice as much work as all the other slaves."

"And after all we did to help him too," said Hector.

"What can I say?" Said Shuffler proudly. "The sultan recognised my many talents and decided to give me a proper paid job!" He turned to Aurnia. "You should have fled when you had the chance. Now you will be a slave as well. As there are now more of you working in this tunnel I think I shall triple the amount of salt I expect to be delivered each day!"

"Oh, so you want a lot of salt, huh?" Muttered Aurnia as she raised her staff in the air. "Then have this!"

Aurnia pointed the staff at the far wall and cast a bolt of lightning. Huge chunks of salt exploded and fell down from the wall, crashing straight into Shuffler and sending him rolling back down the tunnel.

"Come along!" Cried the princess. "Let's get out of here!" The friends ran down the tunnel in single file with Aurnia leading the way. As she emerged back into the main passageway she saw Shuffler lying half buried under a big pile of salt. Hector dragged him away into an alcove where he would be hidden. By chance Goldenmane and the two jackals were hiding in the same alcove and they quickly re-joined the party.

"Now we need to free the rest of the slaves," said Aurnia.

"But how?" Asked One Flower. "There are so many guards around here, princess friend. I'm not sure even your magical staff would be a match for them."

At that moment a gong sounded from afar and echoed through the passageway. "What's that?" Asked Aurnia.

"That is the lunch bell!" Exclaimed Fenner excitedly. "It means we are due our one meal of the day."

As they watched, slaves began to climb down from the tunnels and file away down the passageway. Their heads were down, their eyes grey and lifeless and it was clear they had given up any hope of freedom.

"Come on," said Fang. "Let's follow them to the central cavern. It's the only time the slaves are all together so if we're going to stir up a revolt this would be a good place to do it."

Chapter Nineteen: The Uprising

As Aurnia and her friends were following the slaves down the passageway, Guselin poked his head out of the knapsack pocket. "Aha! So your stupid idiot friends are back with you, huh?" He taunted. "Well it won't do you any good you know. You are all trapped just as I planned! Oh yes!"

"Hello Guselin," said Lunar pleasantly. "You know I actually kind of missed you."

"Foolish wolf!" Laughed the frog. "You should have fled the mighty Guselin whilst you still had the chance. Guselin is not your friend – oh no, he intends to rule over you! Aha!" And with that he leapt out of the knapsack and straight into a big pile of salt.

"Oh no!" Cried Aurnia.

"Ow! Ow! Ow!" Yelled Guselin as he struggled and kicked out. "The salt! It is hurting my skin!"

"I expect it is," scolded Aurnia as she scooped him up from the salt and poured water over him from her flask. "Salt is very bad for frogs and dries out their skin. I would have thought you would have realised that by now."

"Pah! All part of my plan!" Muttered Guselin sulkily as he climbed back into the knapsack pocket and settled down to sleep.

The friends continued walking with the slaves and eventually came into a huge cavern with wooden tables set in long lines. There were hundreds of slaves gathered in the main hall which was surrounded by stern faced soldiers keeping a close watch on everything. "All these poor people," said Aurnia sympathetically.

"Some of them have been here for years," said Fang. "Ever since the sultan took power and what is more most are here for the stupidest of reasons. Throwing a banana skin on to the street, vagrancy, that sort of thing."

Fenner ran ahead to join the line for food. "How can you think about eating at a time like this?" Said Goldenmane.

"How can I help plan a good escape on an empty stomach more like?" Replied Fenner. "Hey, you should get some of this. You might like it considering you eat grass and straw and all kinds of bland rubbish."

"Pah! I see your time in servitude hasn't humbled you," muttered Goldenmane indignantly.

"Look at all these guards," said Whispera worriedly. "There are far more than I thought."

"But there are far more slaves than guards," said Aurnia hopefully. "And the slaves have pickaxes to match their swords. All they need is a leader!"

Aurnia ran forwards and leapt up on to a nearby table. "Listen to me everyone!" She called in the big voice her mother had taught her. "Your days of enslavement are over! It is time to break free! My friends and I are here to rescue you!"

A few of the slaves turned to look at her in surprise. Everyone else ignored her. Even though Aurnia was shouting, her words could not be heard over the noise and chatter in the chamber.

"You must listen to me!" Continued Aurnia. "We must act fast! The sultan must be overthrown!"

Aurnia saw some soldiers jostling through the crowd of slaves towards her, their swords drawn. "Stop those guards!" She cried. "I am trying to free you!" But the terrified slaves moved quickly out of the way of the guards, who continued to advance towards her.

"Right, time to get serious!" Snapped Aurnia crossly. She pointed the staff at the roof and let forth a huge bolt of lightning that illuminated the room and crashed against the ceiling above, sending small rocks of salt raining down on the people in the cavern. Everyone dived for cover. Some of the salt fell down into the cauldrons filled with gruel which served as lunch for the slaves. "Hey!" Exclaimed Fenner as he rushed forwards and stuck his head in the pot to taste it. "This stuff isn't half bad now!"

"Everyone was paying attention to Aurnia now. The soldiers had stopped in their tracks and were staring at the staff in horror. The eyes of everyone in the cavern were upon the princess.

"My name is Princess Aurnia of Cominaer," boomed Aurnia confidently. "I am new to your desert land but what I have seen of it so far has annoyed me a great deal. The sultan is a vile man who has enslaved his own people for the silliest of reasons. He forces you to work in the mines and hires guards to beat and harass you. The time has come to rise up. Let us free ourselves from this mine, march upon Firehara and depose the sultan once and for all!"

"But how?" Came a frightened voice from towards the back. "We might outnumber the sultan's forces but his men are still too strong and well-armed for us to take on!"

"But there is something else!" Cried Fenner as he leapt up on to the table to join Aurnia. "The princess has the magical staff!"

"And that's not all," added Aurnia. "For I am also the Wolf of the Red Moon!"

"Enough of this nonsense!" Cried an overseer captain as he drew his sword and started rushing towards her. "That silly magic trick will not hold us for long. Come along, men, let us overwhelm them and put this rabble back to work!"

"I think not!" Shouted Aurnia. She gripped the staff as a familiar power rushed through her. There came a blinding flash and a booming crash. The princess was gone. In her place was a huge red lupine in spirit form sailing back and forth through the air. Aurnia was the Wolf of the Red Moon once more.

The overseer captain stopped short at the sight of Aurnia. Then his expression hardened. "Another cheap conjuring trick!" He declared. "I am not fooled at all! Let's get her!" And with that he began to run towards her once more. Some other soldiers joined him and before long there was a sizeable group of them making their way towards Aurnia. The Wolf of the Red Moon rose up into the air, flew forwards and scattered the soldiers like skittles to the astonishment of the assembled slaves.

"Can this be?" Breathed Whispera. "Can we really do it?"

"Just believe, brothers and sisters!" Cried One Flower. He leapt on to a table and sprinkled salt around him in a circle. "Let us all unite as one and lead a peaceful revolution; we are all the living creatures of the spirit creation friends, there is no need for violence! Let no weapons clash on this day!"

Sadly, everybody ignore the camelolean. The slaves now rose up against the guards, taking up their pickaxes and whatever other weapons they could find as they sought out the overseers and soldiers. A great fight ensued. Aurnia, as the Wolf of the Red Moon, charged this way and that, flying through the air as she took on and defeated whole groups of defending soldiers. Goldenmane wheeled back and forth, rearing up and kicking out with his back legs. Meanwhile Lunar and Fang teamed up with the two jackals and fought as one small pack. Fenner arched his back and reversed into the enemy, prickling them with his spikes whilst One Flower stood on the table looking at the scene in despair as he pleaded in vain for a peaceful solution. More guards rushed into the cavern but it was no use. They were vastly outnumbered and the slaves had endured more than enough from them. Soon the soldiers had been forced from the cavern. The slaves came out into the passageway and began to fight them back towards the elevator. Before long the soldiers were overwhelmed and fled into the side tunnels to hide. The slaves rushed forwards and blocked their exits, trapping them within.

"Now lets go and free the slaves on the other levels!" Cried Fang as he led the forward charge to the elevator. Lunar and the two jackals joined him at the front but before they reached the elevator they found Pauna lying on the floor in a daze.

"Brother?" Cried Whispera in alarm. "What happened?"

"I was ambushed," groaned Pauna as he slowly opened his eyes. "Some horrible scaley came and said he was a slave trying to escape but when my back was turned he hit me over the head with a big plank of wood."

"Where is he now?" Demanded Luxin.

"He's at the elevator," muttered Pauna. "If you hurry you might catch him."

"That scaley can only have been Shuffler," said Lunar as they ran towards the elevator.

"It certainly was!" Exclaimed Fang. "Look, there he is now!"

As the lupines rounded the corner they saw the fiendish scaley inside the elevator turning the wheels to make it rise up. "You are too late!" Laughed Shuffler. "Now you will be trapped on the lower level forever!"

As the elevator rose up, Lunar rushed forwards and dived towards it but the scaley turned the wheel quickly and it rose just out of her reach. "So long you foolish rebels!" Taunted Shuffler mockingly. "Let your fate serve as a warning to all those who would dare defy our glorious sultan!"

The lupines tried to use Pauna's wheel at the bottom to bring the elevator back but to their horror they found the scaley had smashed it up with a sledgehammer to make it quite unworkable. "Now what are we going to do?" Groaned Lunar. "Just as we thought we were about to win. How awful."

The wolves and jackals headed back to the cavern where Aurnia and her friends were subduing the last of the soldiers. "Now we can get out of here!" Declared the princess as the last of the overseers fled in terror.

"I'm afraid we can't!" Groaned Lunar, and she explained what had just happened at the elevator with Shuffler.

The Wolf of the Red Moon thought for a moment and then smiled. "Don't worry," she said with confidence. "I have an idea. Stand back everyone!"

Aurnia walked over to the far wall in the cavern and began to dig furiously. She dug upwards, very fast indeed, the salt and rock flying out all around her.

"I can't believe it!" Exclaimed Whispera in astonishment. "Is she actually going to dig us out of here?"

"I would have thought such an act would take an age," said Luxin. "But look how fast she is going!"

The Wolf of the Red Moon used the extraordinary strength and stamina gifted to her by the magic of the spirits to dig as fast as she could. Less than five minutes after starting she had broken through on to the second level, to the astonishment of the slaves and guards.

The slaves poured through the tunnel Aurnia had just dug and attacked the guards on the second level. Soon that level too was secured. As soon as the battle was won the Wolf of the Red Moon dug through to the first level. A similar process occurred, and it was easier this time, for the slaves of the second level had been rallied and were eager to win their freedom. Before she knew it the mines had been secured. Over two thousand slaves were now under the command of the Wolf of the Red Moon.

Chapter Twenty: Confronting The Sultan

"Where's Shuffler?" Demanded Fenner angrily as they emerged into the bright desert sunlight. "I was looking for him on all three levels. Oh! When I get my paws on him…"

"There will be time for that later," cautioned Fang. "Now is the time to march on Firehara whilst we still have the momentum about us."

"Yes, and don't forget I will not be the Wolf of the Red Moon forever," added Aurnia.

Aurnia led her friends and the thousands of slaves out into the desert. It was quite a sight to see and everyone was feeling very confident that the wicked sultan's reign was going to be coming to an end very soon. As they marched the slaves sung a defiant song of battle.

"All these years we've mined away!

Worked as slaves. Not a penny of pay!

Now we won't be beaten down!

On to Firehara! We'll soon take that town!

Through the sand dunes!

The Sultan is doomed!

With the Wolf of The Red Moon!"

Aurnia led the pack with Lunar running by her side. From the desert dunes hundreds of jackals appeared to join Whispera, Luxin and Pauna in the final battle. The walls of Firehara appeared in the distance.

But the soldiers had been given advance warning of the rebellion. The walls were flanked with hundreds of troops and as the rebels drew nearer they let fire with arrows and missiles. "It is no use!" Cried Pauna. "We will be cut down before we get close to the walls at this rate."

"Leave it to me," said Aurnia. The Wolf of the Red Moon charged forwards and flew up into the air at lightning speed, flying on to the battlements of the walls and scattering the archers where they stood. Keeping up the momentum she now swooped down and through the streets, putting her head down and smashing through the main gate to leave it wide open. The rebels charged in and were soon doing battle with the astonished soldiers.

Aurnia charged backwards and forwards, knocking the soldiers back and forth across the streets. The slaves outnumbered the sentries but were nowhere near as well trained and without the help of the Wolf of the Red Moon the rebellion would surely have been doomed. Yet with the lupine princess's help the guards were slowly beaten back and defeated.

As Aurnia was leading the charge in the marketplace she happened to look up towards the palace and saw the sultan standing at his balcony. Like all bullies he was a total coward at heart and would not dare come down into the streets to lead his men in battle. Instead he looked pale and frightened as he yelped orders and threats to his battered soldiers.

"There you are!" Exclaimed Aurnia as she took flight towards him. "I have a score to settle with you!"

The sultan fled back into his chambers. Aurnia flew through the window after him and faced him in the great room of state, backing him into a corner. "You are a truly horrible creature!" Cried Aurnia angrily. "You are a liar, a deceiver and a literal slavedriver! I want you to surrender and abdicate your throne right this minute!"

"Anything! Anything!" Cried the cowardly sultan in terror. He sank to the floor and began to weep.

But at that moment Aurnia felt a tingling sensation come over her as the magic around her began to ebb. She fell to the floor as a bright yellow light enveloped her. When it cleared she was back to being a human princess.

The sultan's expression changed in a moment. "Aha!" He exclaimed gleefully as he leapt to his feet. "It looks like the tables have turned!"

Before Aurnia could react, the sultan hurried over to a ceremonial suit of armour to the side of his chamber and seized hold of a long steel sword. He advanced upon Aurnia, waving the sword back and forth with menace. The princess rolled out of the way just in time as the sultan brought the sword crashing down towards her. She hit against a table and brought a candlestick crashing down on to the floor before her. As the sultan slashed at her again she seized hold of the candlestick and leapt to her feet, weakly parrying the blow from the sword.

"I take it all back!" Cried the sultan as he slashed back and forth with the sword. "I shall not resign after all; rather I shall take the Wolf of the Red Moon hostage and find a way to use that magical power for myself!"

"You will never succeed!" Retorted Aurnia as she dodged out of the way and ineffectually tried to fight back with the candlestick. "Your army has been defeated! You have no chance!"

As the sultan advanced, Aurnia leapt over a settee and threw the candlestick at him. It missed by a long way but distracted him enough that she was able to run to the door on the other side of the room. To her horror she found it was locked and now the sultan was coming at her fast. He was by no means an expert swordsman but this hardly mattered considering Aurnia was unarmed.

Aurnia backed away behind the sultan's throne, hoping to delay him for as long as possible until she could think of something. His slaves had fled but the large feather fan was still lying just behind the throne. In desperation the princess seized it up and brandished it before her. As the sultan came forwards she pushed it into his face and he staggered back and spluttered.

"Ow! That tickles!" Cried the sultan. "Stop it! That's annoying and uncomfortable and I cannot see!"

Aurnia realised this was her chance. She moved forwards with the fan, sending the sultan staggering back. The tyrant dropped his sword and put his hands to his face but it was too late.

He staggered out on to the balcony and tipped over the railing. It was a long way down. Aurnia heard a loud thud. She dropped the fan and went to look over the balcony and saw the sultan lying in a large compost heap at the bottom of the garden. As the sultan tried to get up a group of jackals led by Pauna rushed over to detain him. "It is over!" Cried Pauna jubilantly. "The sultan has been captured! We have won!"

Chapter Twenty-One: A New Era

Word of the sultan's capture quickly spread throughout the city. The remaining soldiers threw down their arms and surrendered. Across Firehara the news spread fast: the slaves were free. The sultan's reign of terror was over.

For most of the city this was a time of great celebration. The population came out on to the streets to celebrate their liberation. For those who had profited from the sultan's tyranny, however, it was time to leave the city fast. The jackals, now welcomed back into the city for the first time in years, guarded the gates to make sure they didn't take anything too valuable with them as they fled.

Aurnia and her friends went into the palace. Whispera approached the princess carrying the magical staff in her mouth which she now dropped at Aurnia's feet.

"Now that the sultan is gone we would like you to rule us in his stead," said Whispera hopefully.

Aurnia smiled. "It is a very touching offer," she said gratefully. "But my home is waiting for me in Cominaer. I must find a way back."

"I thought you might say that," sighed Whispera. "But if you won't rule us who will?"

"What about One Flower?" Suggested Lunar.

"Me?" Replied One Flower in surprise. "Wow, I'm not sure if you're joking, wolf friend, and that's awfully nice of you and everything, but I don't exactly have any stand out leadership qualities."

"I quite agree," replied Goldenmane pompously. "One Flower is very common, even for a camelolean."

"Well why not One Flower?" Said Aurnia. "After all, an easy going leader will be far better than then one who went before!"

"Well if that camelolean is going to be leader I shall have to appoint myself his chief minister to keep a close eye on him," said Whispera firmly.

One Flower readily agreed to this. His first decree was that there was to be a huge party across Firehara lasting at least three days. The business of undoing the damage done by the former sultan could wait another day.

With the party in full swing Aurnia, Fenner and Lunar went out on to the sultan's balcony and looked down at the crowds celebrating in the central square.

"We never did find anybody who could help us did we?" Sighed Lunar. "It seems to me we are in exactly the same place as before and still no closer to finding our way home."

"I was thinking the same thing," said Aurnia sadly. "I suppose now the sultan is gone we can stay a few days and see if we can find anything in the royal library. I would be eager to study that book of spells Goldenmane found as well."

"That sultan was a real bad apple," muttered Lunar bitterly. "I hope we can think of a suitable way to punish him."

"Don't worry, I already have," replied Aurnia with a smile. They turned and looked through the double doors. There was the sultan, now dressed in the uniform of a slave, running around serving Goldenmane who was taking great delight in tormenting him and having him carry out the most humble and ridiculous tasks.

"I decided he could serve Lord Goldenmane for a while," laughed Aurnia. "At least until we are ready to leave here. Hopefully when he finds out what it feels like to be treated the way he's treated so many others he will learn a little humility."

"And what about Shuffler?" Asked Fenner. "I hear the jackals caught him cowering in an empty biscuit barrel shortly after the soldiers surrendered."

"Oh don't worry about him, I've got him serving somebody even worse," laughed Aurnia.

"Even worse?" Replied Fenner. "Who could be worse than Goldenmane?"

"More food! More drink! More dancing!" Came a voice from inside the palace. "Oh yes! Sweep that floor! More fanning! Aha! All part of my plan!"

The friends looked inside. There was Guselin, seated on a silk cushion close to the sultan's throne, ordering the wretched Shuffler about. The scaley looked thoroughly miserable as he ran back and forth trying his best to cater to the frog's every whim. Still, thought Aurnia, it was really nothing less than he deserved.

Aurnia went back inside and enjoyed the party for a little while before returning to the balcony. The moon was full in the sky above them. In the midst of all the celebrations the princess could not help feeling a little sad.

"Sometimes I wonder if we will ever make it back home to Cominaer," sighed Aurnia.

"Why of course we will," said Lunar. "We're bound to find something in the library aren't we? Something that tells us where we are and how to get home? Think of all the books in there, Aurnia. One of them must mention our home. It has to."

"I hope so," replied Aurnia. She looked across the city to the silent desert beyond and thought about the cool forests that surrounded her homeland. She thought about Talee, her home city and its narrow cobblestone streets and the great palace where her mother and father lived. *Mum and dad,* thought Aurnia, *how worried they must be about me. I don't know quite what the future holds but no matter how many trials we might have to undergo on our adventures we can never give up hope. And one day, I just know, we will make it home to Cominaer.*

THE END

Printed in Great Britain
by Amazon

32718023R00126